The Message in the Haunted Mansion

In the Blue Room, the dress fitting began. Bess sat on the armchair in the side nook of the girls' bedroom, taking in the side seams of George's dress. "Please hold still, George," Bess pleaded.

"You're sticking me!" George said.

"If you'd stop wiggling, I wouldn't have to," Bess mumbled through a mouthful of pins.

"I can't stand this much longer," George muttered. She leaned against the paneled wall.

"Lean over a little more," Bess directed her.

George bent further, pushing against the wall.

The oak panels creaked and trembled. Then, with a groan, a secret door slowly swung open.

Nancy Drew
Mystery Stories

Available from MINSTREL Books

122

THE MESSAGE IN THE HAUNTED MANSION

CAROLYN KEENE

A MINSTREL® BOOK

PUBLISHED BY POCKET BOOKS

New York   London   Toronto   Sydney   Tokyo   Singapore

This book is a work of fiction. Names, characters, places and incidents are products of the author's imagination or are used fictitiously. Any resemblance to actual events or locales or persons, living or dead, is entirely coincidental.

A MINSTREL PAPERBACK *ORIGINAL*

 A Minstrel Book published by
POCKET BOOKS, a division of Simon & Schuster Inc.
1230 Avenue of the Americas, New York, NY 10020

Copyright © 1994 by Simon & Schuster Inc.
Produced by Mega-Books, Inc.

ISBN: 0-671-87205-2

First Minstrel Books printing December 1994

10 9 8 7 6 5 4 3 2 1

NANCY DREW, NANCY DREW MYSTERY STORIES, A MINSTREL BOOK and colophon are registered trademarks of Simon & Schuster Inc.

Cover art by Aleta Jenks

Printed in the U.S.A.

Contents

1

Jinxed!

"A Victorian mansion in San Francisco—what could be more romantic?" Bess Marvin sighed.

Her cousin, George Fayne, rolled her eyes. "Bess, you're the only person I know who could find renovating an old house romantic."

Nancy Drew laughed, crinkling her blue eyes and brushing back her reddish blond hair. She sat between her two friends in the backseat of a car on a freeway heading into San Francisco.

"I only wish it *were* romantic. Sometimes I think the mansion is jinxed!" exclaimed the car's driver, Rose Green, a tiny woman with steel gray curls.

Nancy leaned forward. "Have there been accidents, Rose?"

"Now, Nancy," Hannah Gruen gently warned. She was the longtime housekeeper for Nancy and her father, lawyer Carson Drew. "Don't go looking for anything suspicious. We're here to help

1

Rose and Abby with their renovations, not solve another of your mysteries."

Hannah sat beside Rose in the front seat. The two women had been friends for several years. Rose had recently retired from her teaching job in River Heights and moved to San Francisco. She and her niece, Abby, were restoring a dilapidated old Victorian mansion so they could open it as a bed-and-breakfast hotel.

"If there *is* anything mysterious about the accidents, Nancy will find out," Bess promised, pulling her long straw blond hair into a ponytail.

"So what kind of accidents are we talking about?" Nancy asked again.

"Just bad luck," Rose answered. "First we had a gas leak and an explosion. Then the scaffolding collapsed. A pipe burst after that. Supplies we ordered didn't come in. There were other things, too—wallpaper paste that didn't stick, paint that wouldn't dry, furniture polish that turned into a mass of sticky goo . . ."

"How frustrating," Hannah sympathized.

Nancy frowned. "When did the trouble start?"

"Our problems started even before we bought the house, Nancy." Rose sighed. "You see, opening a bed-and-breakfast has been my dream. After I retired, I took my life savings, came out to San Francisco, and hunted for the right Victorian house to buy. But the prices were so high."

"But you finally found the house you wanted," Hannah said encouragingly.

"Yes. The mansion was old and in terrible

shape, but the price was right," Rose said. "I made an offer, and it was accepted. But then someone—the real estate agent never told me who—came in with a higher bid, and I almost lost the house. Luckily, my niece, Abby, volunteered to become my partner. With her money added to mine, we were able to match the other bid, and we got the house."

Rose steered the car off the freeway and onto the city streets. Looking out the window, Nancy saw houses and apartment buildings sparkling with Christmas lights. "Any good places to jog around here?" George asked. Slender, dark-haired George loved anything to do with sports —the exact opposite of her cousin Bess.

Rose nodded. "A big park called the Presidio is just a few blocks from our house. And Golden Gate Park isn't far away either."

As Rose turned onto California Street, they passed a Chinese restaurant on the corner, with a large, brightly lit front window. Rose nodded ahead. "There's the house now."

Nancy craned her neck to see an old wooden building outlined by green-pipe scaffolding. The house's faded brown paint was peeling in long strips, and the front porch leaned at a slight angle. Even the iron ornament on the building's tower—some kind of bird—tilted sadly to one side.

"I can see we have a lot of work ahead of us," George muttered to Nancy as Rose pulled up in the driveway.

Perched on the scaffolding, a man in white coveralls wearing a mask and goggles lifted one hand in a brief wave.

"Hi, Charlie!" Rose called out as she got out of the car.

Charlie pulled himself slowly to his feet and came to the end of the scaffolding, limping as he walked.

Hannah and the girls got out of the car. "Charlie, these are my friends from River Heights—Hannah, Nancy, George, and Bess," Rose said, introducing them. Charlie nodded silently and lifted up his goggles. His eyes were wrinkled at the corners and looked tired.

Bess flinched as Charlie raised a large instrument that looked like a gun. "Oh, sorry," Charlie apologized gruffly. "I use this heat gun to soften the old paint so I can scrape it off."

"Once the house is restored, it will be beautiful," Hannah said admiringly. "With those balconies and all the woodwork and that tower, it's like a gingerbread house."

"That's just what all that fancy trim is called—gingerbread," Rose said. "Builders in the Victorian era loved loads of fussy detail. Those balconies, for instance, aren't functional. They're just for decoration."

Charlie turned back to his work, and Rose led her friends up the sagging steps to the front door. Shoving the warped door open with her shoulder, she flipped on a light switch.

Inside, they stood in a grand entry hall with

gleaming wood paneling. On their lefthand side was a large carved door with a mirror set into it. Two more mirrors were built into the wall over carved wood benches. At the far end of the entry hall, a grand staircase with a carved wood banister swept upstairs. In an arch beneath the stairs, a glass-paned door led to the back parts of the house.

Hannah wheeled around to stare at the front door. "This window is magnificent!" she exclaimed, admiring the flowers painted on a panel of stained glass above the front door.

"It is beautiful, isn't it?" said Rose. "On a sunny day, the stained glass throws a rainbow pattern on the wall. It's really lovely. Now, if we could just find the right chandelier." She nodded toward the ceiling, where electrical wires sprouted from a small hole.

Nancy noticed the canvas covering the floor. "Are you refinishing the floors?" she asked.

Rose shook her head. "Not yet. That will come last, after all the painting and the wallpapering is finished. We've painted and papered several rooms, but we still have so much work to do.

"Originally, we planned to open for Christmas," Rose added. "Now we're six months behind schedule. We have to open for business by next summer, or we won't be able to keep up the mortgage payments." Rose smiled bravely, but Nancy thought she looked worried.

Suddenly a voice rang out. "Welcome, Hannah, Nancy, Bess, George!"

Nancy looked around, wondering where the voice had come from. Then the mirrored door opened, and a heavyset woman about thirty-five years old emerged, carrying a black cat. She wore a full skirt, a peasant shawl, and hoop earrings. A purple scarf was tied over her long red hair.

"This is my niece, Abby," Rose said.

"How did you know it was us?" George asked. "You called our names."

Abby just smiled mysteriously.

"Oh, Abby, don't be so dramatic," Rose scolded her lightly. "It's very simple, George—the mirror in the door is a two-way mirror. I'll show you." Rose turned off the lights in the entry, then went in and turned on the parlor's lights. She pulled the door shut behind her. Through the mirrored door they could see her clearly.

"Wow!" Bess said. "Can I try it?" She slipped through the door into the parlor.

"Actually," Rose said, "you can see through the mirror both ways, depending on which room is lit up. Hannah, turn on the entry light."

As Hannah flipped the light switch, Rose turned off the parlor lights. The mirror showed Nancy, George, and Hannah's reflection again. "Hey, it really works!" Bess's excited voice came from the other side of the door. "I can see all of you. I can even see you making that face, George."

Rose threw open the door. "Come on in," she invited Nancy, George, and Hannah. "This is

6

what they called the first parlor. The second parlor is behind it, through those double sliding doors."

Everyone moved into the parlor. It looked like a crowded antique store, filled with chairs, couches, and small polished tables. "It's a bit cluttered," Rose apologized. "But Louis says this busy look was the Victorian style."

"Louis?" Nancy inquired.

A shy smile spread across Rose's face. "Louis Chandler is an antique dealer and decorator," she explained. "He specializes in the Victorian period. He's been extremely helpful, advising us on decor."

Nancy sensed that Louis was someone special to Rose. "How did you meet him?" she asked.

"He just arrived at our door one day," Rose replied. "He welcomed us to the neighborhood and let us know about his shop and decorating services. We can't afford them, but he has kindly given us his help anyway. He's been wonderful!"

"And very attentive," Abby added, giving Rose a teasing nudge with her elbow.

"Abby, please," Rose protested.

Abby had a pot of tea ready, and she poured each of their guests a cup. Bess took hers and stretched out on a velvet chaise longue. "This is *soooo* comfortable. Is there much more work to do indoors? It seems all finished."

"We made a lot of progress this fall," Rose said, "despite the accidents. We got the wiring and plumbing done months ago and then did some carpentry work. Then we started wallpapering and painting. We did the kitchen, a bathroom, and our two bedrooms first, so that we could live comfortably while finishing the rest."

"Now the first parlor is done, the entry, and four of the ten guest rooms," Abby said. "The second parlor is nearly done—I just finished the wallpaper there. After that, there's the dining room, the saloon, and the other six guest rooms."

"The saloon?" George looked puzzled.

Rose nodded. "In the basement, there's a big room that's like an old-time saloon. It even has a built-in bar. You see, we think the house was once a hotel. It's hard to tell, because the floor plan was apparently changed when it became a private home. Two sisters—the Armstrong sisters— owned the mansion for years. They died recently. We bought the house from their nephew, who had no interest in it."

"I looked up the property in one of the old block books at the library, which show all the old lots," Abby said. "I found out that the land was owned back in the late 1800s by an E. Valdez. But we haven't had time to do more research."

"We'll have to go back to the library soon," Rose said. "We need to learn the house's history so we can print up brochures for the bed-and-breakfast. People who stay in B-and-Bs are usually interested in old houses and history. The library has several city documents from before the 1906 earthquake, although most records were destroyed in all the fires that broke out after the earthquake."

"I've been using the library to research old San Francisco theaters, too," Abby added, stroking her cat. "I'm planning an act for the saloon and a séance for Sunday afternoon teas."

Bess's blue eyes widened. "Séance?"

Abby smiled. "Séances were very popular in the last century, Bess. There's a lot we can learn from people in other dimensions."

"Uh, yeah," Bess said vaguely. It was hard to tell whether Abby was serious or not, Nancy thought.

"Maybe we can help you with your research as well as with the renovation work," George offered.

Rose smiled gratefully. "Thanks so much. We're so far behind, especially with the outside work," she said. "The heavy rains this fall really held us up. Charlie's had a lot of work to do, repairing the wooden trim. Now he's beginning to scrape the paint. We'll actually start painting in a few months, when the weather improves."

"We'll do all we can to help," Nancy stressed.

"Thank you, Nancy," Rose said gratefully. "This hotel is my dream. I can't lose it."

Abby patted her aunt's hand. "Why don't we show the girls to their rooms?" she suggested.

"Oh, first can I take a photo?" Bess asked. Pulling her instant camera out of her shoulder bag, she quickly posed the group and snapped a photo. As the picture started to develop, Hannah frowned. "What's that white cloud?" she asked.

Bess stared at the white mist at the top of the photo. "Why . . . it looks like a ghost!"

"Probably a reflection of light," Nancy said.

"Why don't we ask Emily about it when we see her?" Hannah suggested. Hannah's friend Emily Foxworth was a photojournalist. Nancy and George had met her on a previous case in San Francisco.

Bess put the camera away, and Rose led her visitors up the grand staircase. "Eventually," Rose explained, "each bedroom will have its own theme: the Chinese Room, the Spanish Room, the Peacock Room, and so on. That was the Victorian custom. Hannah, you'll be sleeping in the Captain's Room. You girls will share the Chinese Room."

"Oohh," Bess murmured as they entered their bedroom. The Chinese Room was exquisite, with red silk wallpaper and Chinese brush paintings. In the center stood a large ornate bed carved with dragons. A cot had been set up to one side.

"It looks like a movie set," George said.

"The air seems a little stuffy," Rose commented. "Why don't you open a window?"

Bess went over to the room's big arched window. She slid the window up easily and leaned way out, looking up and down California Street.

"The bathroom's down the hall, but there's a sink here in the corner if you want to wash up," Rose told Nancy and George.

Just then Nancy heard a snapping noise. Glancing toward the window, she saw it jerk sharply.

She leapt toward Bess, grabbing her arm and pulling her back. "Wha—" Bess began.

But her voice was cut off as the window came crashing down, shattering glass across the floor.

2

Accident or Foul Play?

Bess stared at Nancy, her eyes huge with fright. "That window could have cut me in two!" she cried.

Both girls were covered with splinters of glass. Large jagged pieces lay on the floor around them. Bess had dropped her teacup, and dark tea stains were spreading across her ivory-colored dress.

Rose ran over, her face ashen. "Are you girls all right?" she asked anxiously.

Nancy and Bess nodded.

"I don't understand," Rose said. "Charlie just repaired these windows. He even replaced the glass." She looked at the damage in dismay. "I'll ask him to clean up and board up the window," she said, quickly leaving the room.

Nancy shook the splinters of glass from her pants, and Bess did the same from her dress. Kicking aside shards of glass, George crossed the room to take a look at the window. Nancy joined her.

"See anything, Nancy?" George asked.

Nancy didn't answer right away. She examined the broken sash cords in the window frame, then crouched down for a better look at the sharp glass fragments. "I don't think this was an accident," she said at last.

Bess looked up in confusion. "You mean it was done on purpose? But how?"

"Even if the cords holding the window frame broke, the glass inside the frame should have held," Nancy said. "There should be putty to hold the glass in. And there ought to be glazing points, too—little metal pieces set between the glass and the window frame. There aren't any." Nancy pointed at the evidence on the floor.

"And look at this," Nancy went on, pointing to the window cords. "Both sash cords are broken. Even if they were old, they wouldn't both break at the same time. And if this was natural wear and tear, the cords would be frayed. These have been cut clean through."

"Someone *wanted* the window to fall," said George uneasily.

Nancy nodded slowly. "I think so. And here's another thing." Nancy stood up and held out her hands.

Bess touched Nancy's fingers. "Ew! Your fingers are all slippery. What's on them?"

"Some kind of lubricant from the cords," Nancy said. "They've been oiled to make them slippery. Someone wanted the window to fall fast

13

and hard, so the glass would shatter. This was no accident."

"What about the other accidents Rose told us about?" Bess said slowly. "Do you think they were deliberate, too?"

Nancy shrugged and returned to the window. "That's what we have to find out."

"But who would do this?" George asked. "Could it have been Charlie? Rose said he had just repaired the window."

"He's the logical suspect," Nancy admitted. "We don't have any proof or any motive for him. But we'd better find out fast. If these accidents continue, Rose or Abby might get hurt."

They heard a knock, and Hannah came in. "Rose told me about the accident," she said, looking worried. "Were you girls hurt?"

"We're all fine, Hannah," Nancy assured her.

Hannah shook her head. "Poor Rose. There's just one problem after another in this old house." She looked at Nancy. "We need to keep Rose's spirits up. I suggested she take us for a drive and show us some sights. You'll all come along, won't you?"

The girls agreed, but Bess said she needed to change her clothes first. "I want to soak my dress right away so the tea stains don't set," she said.

Nancy and George went downstairs to explore the house until Bess, Rose, and Hannah were ready to leave.

Behind the glass door at the rear of the entry hall, they found two small anterooms, like little

14

hallways. From the first one, a broad carpeted staircase led down into darkness. From the second, a narrow set of worn wooden stairs led up.

"I bet this used to be the servants' stairway," said George, peering up the narrow staircase. "And maybe these other stairs lead down to the basement saloon."

Nancy fingered a latch on the inside of the door that led to the downward staircase. "It's odd that the latch would be on this side of the door," she commented. "Maybe the hotel owner needed to lock off the saloon during certain periods of the day. Anyway, let's go down and look at it."

She and George made their way slowly down the dark staircase. At the bottom, the stairs opened into a huge room. A little sunlight filtered in through small, high ventilation windows.

The saloon seemed to run the length of the house. A long bar with a mirror behind it stretched across one end. A few tables and chairs, a small stage, and a grand piano occupied the room.

Nancy and George walked over to the mahogany bar. "What a beautiful mirror," Nancy said, pointing at the bar's huge mirror, which had birds and flowers etched into its frame.

In the mirror, Nancy saw a movement behind her. She turned to spot Abby slipping furtively away from the piano. "Abby!" said Nancy in surprise.

Abby whirled around. "When did you girls come in?" she asked sharply.

"Just now," said Nancy, wondering at Abby's rude tone. "What are—" Nancy's question was interrupted by a honking horn outside.

"That's probably Rose. It must be time for you to go," Abby said.

She's trying to get rid of us, Nancy thought.

"Aren't you coming with us, Abby?" George asked.

"No," Abby said in a testy voice.

"Well, we'll see you soon, then," Nancy said. She and George headed for the saloon stairs. When Nancy looked back, Abby was still standing in the center of the room, watching them.

Upstairs in the entry hall, George said softly to Nancy, "What was Abby doing down there? She definitely wasn't happy to see us."

"I thought the same thing," Nancy murmured.

George grinned. "Uh-oh. You've got that let's-figure-out-this-mystery look," she said.

Nancy smiled. "Guilty."

They stepped outside, where Rose, Hannah, and Bess were waiting in Rose's red car. George climbed into the backseat with Bess.

Just as Nancy was about to follow, something caught her eye across the street. A blond teenage boy wearing an old army jacket stood on the sidewalk, hands jammed into the pockets of his ragged jeans. When he saw Nancy notice him, he turned swiftly and walked away.

Nancy narrowed her eyes and watched him go up the street. Then she climbed into Rose's car.

Rose drove her guests through the Alamo

Square Historic District, where there were many Victorian houses painted in all the colors of the rainbow. At a tall hill called Twin Peaks, they got out of the car to admire a panoramic view of the city.

They drove back through huge Golden Gate Park, with its museums, playing fields, lakes, and wooded areas. Rose pointed out an enormous tent standing in a meadow. "That's the pavilion for the Winter Festival next Sunday," she said. "Louis is on the planning committee. We're going to help at his booth."

Next, Rose suggested they stop for an early supper. She took them to the Land's End Inn, a popular spot set atop a rocky cliff overlooking San Francisco Bay. "What a view," Hannah said, pausing on their way inside. "But you couldn't get me in that water. It must be freezing!"

Indoors, Hannah and Rose made a quick stop at the powder room. While waiting for them, the girls wandered through an exhibit on old San Francisco in the restaurant's lobby.

"Look at this," Bess called to Nancy and George. They joined her in front of a group of antique photographs. All the pictures on that part of the wall showed a full-figured woman with blond curls. Bess was reading a framed article on the wall next to the pictures.

"This is Lizzie Applegate. She was an entertainer in the gold mining camps," Bess said. "A bandit called El Diablo fell in love with her. Then one day Lizzie disappeared, and apparent-

17

ly she joined the bandit's gang in robbing stage-coaches!"

Nancy and George grinned at each other. They knew Bess loved any kind of romantic story.

"What happened to Lizzie?" Nancy asked.

"She showed up in San Francisco and became an actress," Bess said, scanning the article. "She wrote a play called *The Bandit's Treasure* about an outlaw just like El Diablo. Later she opened a hotel, but it burned down in a fire. Gee, I would love to live a life as exciting as hers!"

"Oh, really?" George eyed her cousin skeptically. "Camping out with a gang of thieves in the wilderness? No bath or shower for weeks at a time?"

"Maybe not that part," Bess admitted. "But I'd like the part when the bandit fell in love with Lizzie and when she became a famous actress."

Soon Hannah and Rose returned, and the five of them were seated at a window table. They watched a gorgeous sunset while they ate a light dinner of soup and salad.

When they got back to the mansion, just after seven, a silver sedan was parked out front. "Louis is here!" said Rose, her face lighting up. "Wait until you meet him, Hannah." Rose quickly checked her hair and makeup in the rearview mirror.

Inside, the mirrored door to the first parlor was open. As they walked in, Nancy saw Abby and Charlie standing in the second parlor, staring at one of the walls. Beside them was a silver-haired man dressed in a dark gray suit.

"Louis," Rose began, moving forward with a big smile. "I want you to meet—" Suddenly she stopped and gave a cry.

Nancy, Bess, and George followed her into the second parlor to see what Abby, Charlie, and Louis were staring at.

The wall was sopping wet from floor to ceiling, with water still trickling down it. The rose-patterned wallpaper hung down in strips.

Abby turned and glared at the girls in fury.

"What happened?" Nancy asked.

Charlie muttered something, then limped from the room. Louis turned to Rose. "Charlie came in to board up the window in the Chinese Room," he said. "He found a flood there. The water went through the floor and ran down here."

Abby's eyes were flashing. "I went out," she spat out. "When I came back . . . destroyed! I just spent the whole afternoon wallpapering, and now all my work is ruined!"

"But how did this happen?" Nancy asked again.

"*Someone* left the water running in *your* room upstairs," Abby sputtered angrily. "The sink overflowed. *Someone didn't remember to turn off the faucet!*"

Nancy's heart sank. She recalled that Bess had been soaking her dress upstairs just before they left the house. She looked over at Bess.

Bess's eyes grew wide. "No!" she protested. "No! I know I turned off the water. I know I did!"

19

3

The Figure in the Fog

Bess's frightened eyes traveled from Nancy and George to the wet wallpaper to Abby. "I turned off the water! You have to believe me!"

"Of course we believe you, Bess," Nancy said, giving Bess's hand a little squeeze.

"Yes, Bess, of course. It's just . . ." Rose faltered, looking around helplessly. Finally she tottered back into the first parlor and sank down onto one of the couches, covering her face with her hands. "What next?" she whispered.

Coming to sit beside Rose, Louis took her hands in his and began to speak to her softly. Abby stormed up behind them.

"Rose," Abby said sharply. "They can't stay in the Chinese Room now. The carpet up there is soaked through, and there's glass all over the floor. But we have no other room ready for them to sleep in."

Nancy had the feeling that Abby would have

liked to send them back to River Heights on the next plane.

"The girls can stay in my room with me," Hannah offered quickly.

Rose lifted her head. "The Blue Room has that big bed in it," she said, her voice weary. "The room hasn't been painted yet, but it's clean."

Abby threw up her hands. "Fine, the Blue Room then," she said to the girls. "There's only one bed, but it's a large four-poster. Two of you can share it, and we can move the cot. Follow me."

In silence, Nancy, George, and Bess trooped behind Abby, heading up the stairs and down the hall. Abby stopped at a linen closet, yanking out pillows, sheets, a blanket, and a quilt. Without a word, she thrust them at Nancy and George, ignoring Bess's open arms.

Down the hall, right next to the flooded Chinese Room, she opened another door. "The Blue Room," she said. "You can bring your bags over." Then Abby strode away.

"That's what I call the silent treatment," Bess complained, her voice quavering. "She wouldn't even *look* at me." Nancy slipped a comforting arm around her friend's shoulders.

The Blue Room was clean, but that was about it. Strips of faded blue wallpaper hung down off the walls. The floor had bare, worn boards. The furniture was all antiques—a four-poster bed, a dark wood bureau topped with green marble, and a large mirror. Through an arch on one side, a small nook held a writing desk and a shabby armchair.

George tossed a sheet at Bess. "Make yourself useful, cousin," she said. "And stop worrying. *We* know you didn't leave that water on."

Nancy stuffed a pillow into a pillowcase. "I doubt the flood was an accident anyway," she declared.

Bess looked up from the sheet she and George were spreading across the large mattress. "What do you mean?" she asked.

"I think someone deliberately turned on the tap in the sink," Nancy explained.

"But who?" George said.

"Abby and Charlie both were here," Nancy noted.

"Abby? Why would she sabotage her own house?" George asked, grabbing the blanket.

"I don't know," Nancy admitted. "But she was sure in a hurry to blame us for the flood." She paused, thinking. "What we need is a motive. We need to figure out why anyone would want to create these accidents."

Bess tucked in the blanket at the foot of the bed. "Remember when Rose told us that someone else made an offer for the house?" she said. "Maybe that other person wants the house so bad, he or she is trying to drive Rose and Abby out."

"Good point, Bess," Nancy said. "Someone may really want the bed-and-breakfast project to fail, so they're staging a series of phony accidents to make Rose and Abby give up and sell the house."

"But, Nancy, there must be other Victorian mansions," George said. "Why this one?"

Nancy shrugged. "Maybe there's something about this house we don't know," she mused.

Bess clasped her hands together. "Yes! Some mysterious, tragic secret from the past!"

"Oh, please," George scoffed.

Nancy smiled. "I think Bess is right—in principle anyway," she said. "Maybe there *is* some secret about this house."

"Rose said it was once a hotel," George said.

"E. Valdez owned the land in the 1800s," Bess remembered. "Then the Armstrong sisters lived here."

"How can we find out more?" George asked.

"We could go to the library," Nancy answered. "And I bet Louis can help us. He's an expert on the Victorian period."

"Sounds good. Let's go find Louis," said George, heading for the door.

Bess held up a hand to stop her. "Uh, before we dive into research, how about diving into something to eat?" she suggested. "That salad at the restaurant was good, but it wasn't exactly filling."

"Actually, I'm a little hungry myself," George admitted. "Let's check out what's in the kitchen."

Bess winced. "I'd hate to ask for food right

now," she said. "Rose is upset, and Abby's mad at me. But how about that Chinese restaurant we saw on the corner?"

"Sounds good," George agreed. "Let's just move the cot first."

When the girls finally went downstairs, they found Rose and Hannah in the kitchen. Louis had just left, and Hannah was baking blueberry muffins for breakfast. The two older women smiled when they heard the girls were hungry again and told them to enjoy their Chinese food.

It was a short walk to the restaurant. When they entered, Nancy immediately felt as if she were in another country. Chinese scrolls decorated the walls, and the tables were set with elegant sea green china. But the focal point of the room was an immense mantel set over the fireplace, painted a Chinese red. With its large wings and ornately carved wood, the mantel looked like a pagoda, an ornate entrance to some mysterious temple.

"Look at the woodwork on that bird," Bess said, nodding at the graceful bird carved into the wood at the top of the mantel.

"Hey, Nancy, it's a phoenix," George said.

"A phoenix?" Bess asked.

Nancy nodded. "A mythical bird," she explained to Bess. "Supposedly, after living five hundred years, it set fire to itself and died, then rose from the ashes to live again."

Bess raised her eyebrows. "Been thumbing through the encyclopedia again?" she teased.

Nancy laughed. "Lieutenant Chin told George and me about the phoenix when we worked with him on Emily Foxworth's case," she said. "It's a San Francisco symbol. In its early years, the city burned many times, but each time it was rebuilt, just like the phoenix rising from the ashes. You'll notice that the police wear a phoenix symbol on their uniforms."

Nancy, Bess, and George ordered their meal. As they were finishing, a teenage girl in a pink sweatsuit and running shoes came to their table to clear the dishes. Her long black hair was pulled back under a sweatband and her face was flushed. "Just been out running?" George asked her.

The girl grinned and nodded. "My mom hates me to work in my running clothes," she said, "but sometimes I barely have enough time to get in a run, much less shower and change."

George smiled. "I know what you mean," she said. "Say, maybe we could run together sometime. We're staying right down the street."

"That'd be great! I'm Mary Lee," the girl said. "My family owns the restaurant. I work here part-time while I go to school. When are you—"

Suddenly she stopped, her eye caught by something out the front window.

Nancy followed Mary's gaze. Outside was the same blond teenage boy she had seen earlier.

Seeing Mary, the boy gave a little wave. Mary saw him, bobbed her head, then threw him a meaningful glance toward Nancy, George, and Bess.

Mary looked flustered all of a sudden. "Um, what was—oh, yes, your check," she said distractedly, lifting a stack of dishes. She spun around and hurried off to the kitchen.

Nancy looked back out the window, but the boy had disappeared. It was obvious that Mary knew him, Nancy thought. But why did she react so strangely when she saw him?

But when Mary Lee brought their bill, she acted as if nothing had happened. She and George exchanged phone numbers. The girls paid the bill and then left.

As they returned to the mansion, a thick fog was rolling in, shrouding the neighborhood in a white mist.

Inside, the house was filled with the smell of Hannah's blueberry muffins. The girls trooped up to the Blue Room, exhausted by their long day. Bess and George changed for bed right away. Nancy headed down the hall for the bathroom.

Nancy had finished brushing her teeth and was just leaving the bathroom when she halted. A soft hissing noise seemed to be coming from outside the bathroom window. What was it? she wondered.

Nancy carefully raised the small window. Above the noise of car traffic, muffled by the fog, she could hear a dog barking but nothing else.

Then she saw it. Floating outside a window to her right was a silvery white figure, half lost in the fog. It looked almost like a body—or a ghost. "Who is it?" Nancy called.

There was another soft hiss, and then the figure disappeared. Nancy heard a thud.

She waited for the apparition to reappear, but she could see nothing through the dense fog. Then a light shone out from the window right where the floating figure had been.

Shutting the window, Nancy crept out into the dimly lit hallway, heading toward her left. She stopped outside a door with a crack of light shining underneath. She knocked softly.

After a few moments, the door opened and Abby appeared in a black velveteen robe. "Oh, Nancy," she said, surprised. "Is anything wrong?"

"I just saw something. I think it was outside your window," Nancy told her. "I'm not sure what it was."

Abby smiled, arching her eyebrows. "The same thing happened when I first moved here," she said. "I thought I saw all kinds of things I couldn't explain. There's definitely an aura about this house. But I'm sure there's nothing outside my window."

"I definitely saw something, Abby," Nancy insisted. "Could we take a look?"

Abby's smile dropped. She looked back over her shoulder, hesitating. "All right, but quickly," she said.

Nancy followed Abby across her bedroom. The

decor certainly was dramatic, Nancy thought—a rich-looking red-and-black patterned carpet, red flocked wallpaper, large gilt mirrors, even black satin sheets and a quilted red bedspread. Alfreida, Abby's black cat, darted under the bed.

Leaning out the window, Nancy heard the barking dog again, but she could see nothing else. She pulled her head back in, puzzled.

"I told you," Abby said. "It was just your imagination." As she shut the window, it made the same thudding sound Nancy had heard a minute earlier. "Now, if you don't mind, I was about to go to sleep," Abby said pointedly.

Nancy noticed Alfreida pawing at a piece of shiny cloth sticking out from under the bed. But then Abby walked in front of Nancy, cutting off her view of the cat. She motioned to the door, a fixed smile on her face.

"Good night," Nancy said. Unable to invent a reason to stay in Abby's room, she went back to the Blue Room.

Bess and George were sitting up in bed. Nancy told them what had happened.

"You saw a ghost!" Bess declared.

"I think that's what Abby wants me to think, with her talk about 'auras,'" Nancy reasoned. "But what I saw wasn't a ghost, and whatever it was, Abby knows something about it."

"Nancy, maybe that's the secret of this house—a ghost who doesn't want anybody to live here. Maybe it was some young girl who died of a broken heart, and her ghost walks each night!"

Flinging one hand theatrically to her forehead, Bess kneeled on the bed, pretending to die of heartbreak. She gripped the bedpost with the other hand.

Suddenly the bedpost knob came off in Bess's hand. "Whoops!" Bess said, thrown off balance and nearly falling off the bed.

Bess sprang back to screw the knob back on the bedpost. But as she began to fit it onto the peg, she stopped and stared inside the hollow post. Then she gasped.

"Nancy! George! A key!"

4

A Surprise Ending

"Maybe this key will unlock the secrets of this house!" Bess said excitedly. She pulled a big, old-fashioned key from the hollow recess in the bedpost.

George scrambled over to take a look at it. "But what lock does it fit?" she wondered.

Nancy examined the key. "If we can find out where the bed came from, that may tell us what the key is for," she said. "Bess, put the key in the bureau for safekeeping right now. And let's not mention finding the key to anyone just yet—not until we understand what's going on in this house."

Nancy couldn't remember falling asleep, but when she opened her eyes, it was daylight. She dressed quietly, slipping on jeans and a hooded sweatshirt. Just as she was leaving the bedroom, George began to stretch and Bess blinked open her eyes.

"I'll meet you sleepyheads downstairs," Nancy said. "And I'll *try* to save some of Hannah's blueberry muffins for you."

Bess yawned and rubbed her eyes. "I was just dreaming that I was Lizzie Applegate and I was an actress in San Francisco," she said.

"You're in San Francisco, all right," George teased, "but the only acting you're doing is pretending you aren't hungry for those muffins."

As she left the room, Nancy saw Abby slip through a door about halfway down the hall. Nancy started to follow but stopped when she spotted Charlie repairing the window in the Chinese Room. Now would be a good time to question him, she thought.

From the doorway, Nancy watched him fit the new window pane into the frame. Then he reached for his putty knife, one of several tools hanging from his leather belt. As he turned his head, he saw Nancy.

"Good morning, Charlie," she said.

"Morning," he replied gruffly.

"Gee, Charlie, what would make a window crash down like that with such terrific force?" Nancy asked, trying to sound innocently curious.

Charlie gave Nancy an odd look. Then he shrugged. "Crummy cords, that's all," he muttered.

Nancy frowned. Was Charlie lying or had he really not noticed that the cords had been cut? Why hadn't he replaced the old cords when he repaired the window the first time? And why hadn't he used putty and glazing points to hold the window in place before? He was using putty today.

Nancy decided to try to get Charlie talking. The more she knew about him, the better her chance of finding out what he knew about the "accidents." "What work can we do today?" she asked.

"If you really want to help," he said over his shoulder, "a couple of you girls could chip off the old paint on the woodwork outside. Then I'll show you how to sand and prime the wood."

"Have you restored a lot of Victorian houses?" Nancy asked, coming closer.

Charlie shrugged, continuing to work. "Sure, when I can. I love these old houses. But the work isn't steady. Can't make it without a second job."

"But there are so many Victorians," Nancy said. "I'd think there would be plenty of jobs around."

"Plenty of people needing work, too," he said. "Besides," he added bitterly, "a lot of people won't hire an old guy like me, an old guy with a limp. They think I can't do the job."

"Well, you've certainly done good work here," Nancy said. "The woodwork in the entry hall, for example—it's spectacular."

Charlie turned to her. "Why, thanks," he said in a softer voice. "It takes time, but you've got to do it right. It's like I owe it to the guys who did the work so well the first time around."

"Well, we're happy to help," Nancy said kindly. "I hope we can do the house justice."

Charlie nodded and returned to his work. Nancy headed back down the hall, stopping by the door she'd seen Abby use a moment ago. She opened it and found the servants' staircase. She went downstairs and found Rose in the kitchen, slicing apples into a large bowl of fruit salad.

"Good morning, Nancy," Rose said cheerfully. "Did you girls sleep all right?"

"We sure did," Nancy said. "That bed in the Blue Room is comfy, and it's so beautiful. Where did you find it, by the way?" she asked casually, hoping for some clue about the key Bess had found.

"That was in the house when we bought it," Rose said. "It's so big, I imagine there's no way to move it out of that room. I suspect it was built right there, in fact."

Just then Bess and George trooped in from the front hall, dressed in jeans and sweatshirts. Bess eyed Rose's fruit salad. "I'm starving!" she said.

"Still hungry?" Rose said playfully. "After gobbling up a platterful of muffins?"

Nancy, George, and Bess looked at her in confusion. "Hannah's muffins?" Bess asked. "I've been looking forward to them. Where are they?"

Rose looked confused. "Why, when I came down this morning, they were all eaten. I thought you girls were the culprits."

Nancy, Bess, and George shook their heads.

"But if you didn't eat them, who did?" Rose asked. "Hannah said she didn't, and so did Abby—I asked them both."

"What about Charlie?" Nancy asked, curious.

"Oh, Charlie hardly ever takes time out to eat," Rose declared. "Besides, he wouldn't steal anything. He's really a good person. Maybe he seems a little grouchy, but that's just because he feels bad that this project is so far behind. You know, he's even charging us lower rates for his work since he saw we were getting tight on money."

Nancy nodded, but to herself she thought, Is Rose right about Charlie? Or is she just someone who always thinks the best of other people? One thing was sure: If Charlie was causing the "accidents," Rose didn't suspect it.

Rose leaned against the counter, pondering. "Come to think of it," she went on, "this isn't the first food that's disappeared. About a week ago, I bought a pie. Half of it was eaten during the night. I assumed it was Abby, but I didn't ask her. She's kind of sensitive about her weight."

"I can sympathize with that," Bess murmured.

"Well, it doesn't matter," Rose said briskly, wiping her hands on a tea towel. "Can you girls help me carry breakfast into the dining room?"

Though the dining room wasn't finished yet, Rose had set up a small table there. The girls helped her carry out fruit salad, buttered toast, a pitcher of orange juice, and a pot of hot coffee.

George unhooked the latch on one of the

34

dining room windows and began to raise it. "Hey, look," she said in surprise. "The wall's attached to the window!" She pointed to the lower wall paneling, which was sliding upward along with the window.

"Ah, I see you've discovered the jib door," Rose said. "What looks like a window is actually a door that slides up and down."

"What's it for?" George asked.

"Look how large an opening you have when the jib door is open," Rose pointed out. "It's like having an extra door at the back of the house. It helps when you're moving furniture in. And speaking of moving—while we're waiting for Hannah and Abby to join us, can you help me move something?"

"Sure thing," said Nancy. "What?"

Rose pointed at several large ceramic crocks in the corner of the dining room. "We bought these to store flour, sugar, and oatmeal," she said. "Someday we'll be serving big breakfasts every day—*when* we open for business." She grimaced. "But it's obviously going to be months until then. I'd like to move these crocks into the pantry for now to get them out of the way."

"No problem," Nancy said. The girls each lugged a heavy crock into the pantry and set them against one wall.

Just then the front doorbell rang. Rose hurried out to answer it. "Why, hello, Louis!" the girls heard her call out happily. "You're just in time for breakfast. Come on into the dining room."

35

Nancy, Bess, and George returned to the dining room as Rose entered with Louis Chandler. "I'm afraid we weren't introduced properly, what with all of the excitement yesterday," he greeted them pleasantly. Louis gave each girl a firm handshake as Rose introduced him.

Louis took off his cashmere muffler and overcoat. He looked quite distinguished with his crisp white shirt, silk handkerchief, and well-cut dark suit. Placing his briefcase on the table, Louis opened it to show Rose some brochures advertising the next Sunday's Winter Festival in Golden Gate Park. "I'm very grateful to you and Abby for offering to help at my booth," he said.

"It's the least we can do to repay you after all the help you've given us," Rose said.

Louis covered Rose's hand with his. "Your friendship is repayment enough, Rose," he said. "But then, I think you know that," he added softly, leaning toward her. A glow spread over Rose's face.

"Uh, what kind of festival will it be?" Bess asked, interrupting the twosome.

"A holiday arts and crafts fair," Louis told her. "And there will be music, dancing, and refreshments. Various artists and small shop owners like me will display their wares in their booths. Since my merchandise is all Victorian antiques, I'm trying to convince Rose to dress as a Victorian lady."

"Ooh! Do you need anyone else to help?" Bess

spoke up promptly. "Nancy, George, and I could wear Victorian costumes, too."

George shot Bess a stony look, but Louis seemed very pleased at Bess's offer.

"Why, yes, that would be grand," he said. "There are several vintage clothing stores on Sacramento Street, near my store," he said. "You ought to be able to find some suitable costumes."

"Speaking of helping out," Nancy put in, "we'd like to help Rose and Abby research this house's history. Any suggestions on where we could start?"

Louis rubbed his jaw, considering. "It's hard to say, Nancy," he said. "The fires after the 1906 earthquake destroyed just about all the records."

"Why, Louis," Abby said, suddenly appearing in the doorway, "the public library has lots of old records—old telephone directories, insurance maps, that kind of thing. Last time I was there, I picked up a booklet on how to research your house at the library."

"Yes, yes, you're right, Abby," Louis said hastily. "The library does have a lot of old records. But perhaps you girls ought to focus on the work here first before getting bogged down in time-consuming research. Rose and Abby really need your help here at the house."

"But, Louis," Rose said, looking puzzled, "I've been wanting to get this research done since we bought the house. We should have a full history of the house put together before we open. You told me that yourself."

"Well, yes, of course, but—" Louis started. Then his smile returned. "I guess I'm just so eager to see the physical work on the house completed. But I agree, it might be useful to have the girls visit the library." He waved a hand briskly. "Sorry, I can't stay for breakfast, Rose, but an important client is coming to the shop."

Louis placed his brochures back in his briefcase and kissed Rose on the cheek. Rose blushed and Louis laughed. "That's my blushing Rose," he said. Rose blushed even more.

Rose walked Louis to the door. Nancy frowned as she watched them go. She felt sure that Louis had known the library held those documents. Why was he trying to prevent them from doing the research?

After breakfast Abby, Hannah, and Bess went to work in the second parlor, stripping off the wallpaper that had been soaked the day before. "It's the least I can do," Bess said. "Even though I know I didn't cause the flood."

Abby threw her a forgiving glance. "Don't worry about it, Bess," she said. "We believe you."

Nancy and George went outside to help Charlie. The day was overcast, gray, and cold. Sitting on planks up on the scaffolding, Nancy and George began chipping the thick paint from the woodwork on the upper gable. By noon their arms ached. When they stopped for lunch, they took off their work gloves and found blisters on their fingers.

By the end of the afternoon, George's arms were sagging. "I'm beat, Nancy," she moaned.

"Me, too," Nancy admitted. "And I'm cold."

Just then Abby shouted up at the girls from the sidewalk below. "As long as you're up there, could you straighten the ornament on the tower?"

Nancy raised her eyes to the top of the tower where the ornamental bird sat, tilting at an odd angle. "Okay!" she called down. Slipping her paint scraper into the pocket of her jeans, she gripped the edge of the roof. She threw one leg up and over the roof's edge, and with aching arms lifted herself up.

She tiptoed across the shingled roof to the tower, holding her arms out for balance. Wrapping her arms and legs around the cone-shaped structure, she began to shimmy her way to the top.

With numb, sore hands, Nancy inched her way up. Finally, she reached out to grasp the wrought-iron bird.

A shout came from below. Nancy looked down and saw Charlie gesturing frantically.

Suddenly Nancy felt the tower roof begin to give beneath her. She spread her arms and legs even wider, trying to distribute her weight better, but it was no use.

The tower gave a final tremble. An instant later, Nancy went crashing through the roof!

5

The Golden Gardenia

Nancy's hands clutched at thin air as she plunged through the roof tower. She landed with a heavy thud, shingles and wood crashing around her. Stunned, Nancy remained motionless as debris kept raining down from the roof. Then everything was quiet.

She unfolded her arms and legs and sat up. Her right hip stung, but a quick check told her she wasn't seriously hurt. Brushing off her face and clothes, she stood up and looked around her.

She'd landed in an unfinished attic space, full of dust and cobwebs. Next to her was a large black trunk. Beside it stood a small green writing desk.

Suddenly Nancy heard George's voice calling out to her. "Nancy! Are you all right?"

Standing on the trunk, Nancy waved an arm through the hole in the roof, hoping George could see her. Then she jumped down and scanned the bare floorboards, hoping to find a

40

door that would lead to the house below. Kicking away the dust, she saw an old rope handle attached to a trapdoor.

Nancy tugged at the handle, but the old rope split in her hands. She pulled the paint scraper from her pocket and edged it around the crack between the door and the floor planks.

A tapping noise came from the room beneath. "Are you all right?" a voice below called.

Nancy recognized Rose's voice. "I'm fine," she called back. The door finally loosened as Nancy pried at it with the scraper. At last it gave way. Nancy opened the door to find Rose staring up at her.

"Oh, Nancy, are you all right?" Rose gasped. "I was in this room, measuring for curtains, when I heard a crash."

"I'm fine," Nancy assured her. "But I don't think the roof's in such great shape."

Just then Hannah and Bess rushed into the room, still holding their glue brushes. When Hannah saw Nancy standing above the trapdoor, she pressed her hand to her heart.

"Thank goodness you're okay!" Hannah exclaimed. "We heard George yell. I didn't know what had happened."

"I told you the roof wouldn't hold weight!" Charlie's angry voice broke in. Nancy saw him rush into the room, too, with Abby and George on either side. "Abby, I told you the other day that no one was to go up there!"

"I thought you meant *I* shouldn't," Abby pro-

41

tested defensively. "But Nancy's so light. I thought maybe she could just straighten the ornament."

"The whole finial—the bird, the base, and everything—needs to be removed and repaired properly," Charlie insisted. "You can't just give the bird a little shove and expect it to stay in position. Nancy could have been killed!"

"I'm fine," Nancy called down. "And I've made a discovery. This tower is an old attic. There's a trunk up here and a little desk, too."

Rose leaned over to peer up through the hole. "Why, we thought the turret was just an ornament, like the false balconies," she said. "We don't have real house plans—they disappeared long ago."

"As long as I'm up here, let's lower the desk and trunk and take a look," Nancy suggested.

"I'll get ropes," Charlie growled.

"And a crowbar," Nancy added. "So we can pry open this trunk."

Soon Charlie returned with his tool kit, several coils of rope, a sheet of heavy plastic, and a staple gun. With his guidance, Nancy fastened the ropes securely around the trunk and small desk. She lowered them slowly through the trapdoor into Charlie's and George's arms. Then she quickly tacked the plastic over the hole and jumped down herself.

"I have to go," Charlie said abruptly, checking his watch. "I have to be somewhere at five." He nodded goodbye and limped away down the hall.

Excited by their discovery, the others hardly noticed his leaving. Bess and George pried open the trunk first to find a pile of elaborate gowns from the 1800s.

"We can wear these dresses to the Winter Festival," Bess cried, holding up a pink brocade gown, then a crimson dress with black trim. "We'll look so incredible!"

George stifled a little groan.

Nancy tried to lift the lid on the small desk. "It's locked," she announced.

"Oh, Nancy, what about the key we found in the bedpost?" Bess suggested. "I'll run and get it." She flew from the room.

Abby looked up, frowning. "What key?"

Wishing Bess hadn't said anything, Nancy told Hannah, Rose, and Abby how they'd found the key.

"I wish you'd told me," Abby scolded. "Rose and I need to know about every nook and cranny of this house."

"Oh, Abby, I'm sure the girls meant no harm," Rose chided her.

Bess returned with the key. They all gathered around as she placed it into the lock. "It fits!" she exclaimed.

Nancy turned the key and lifted the lid. The desk was filled with old papers. She picked up a letter from the top of the pile, scanning the elegant writing. "This letter is dated 1883."

"Let me see," said Bess.

"Be careful," Rose said as Nancy handed it to Bess. "That paper's so old, it's crumbling."

Nancy inspected the other papers in the desk. "I'll bet this desk hasn't been opened since the turn of the century," she marveled. "All the dates on these papers are old: 1897, 1894, 1882. There are notebooks and photographs, too."

"This is like finding a time capsule," George said, gazing at the old documents.

"Maybe these papers will tell us the history of the mansion," Nancy said hopefully.

Rose suggested that they move the small desk down to the first parlor, where they could examine the papers better. Nancy and George carried it downstairs for her.

Because it was dark outside by then, everyone cleaned up and met in the dining room for a quick supper. Then they hurried into the front parlor to open the desk again.

Another fog had rolled in, bringing a damp chill. George built a fire in the fireplace, and Abby and the three girls sat in front of it, spreading the papers from the desk on the carpet.

"Let me know if you find anything juicy," said Rose, settling down at her sewing machine. "I'm going to finish these curtains for the upstairs hall. I've had my fill of leafing through old papers—I went through all my old letters last week to get started on writing my Christmas cards."

"I'll help with the curtains, Rose," Hannah offered.

Bess was flipping through a stack of photographs. "Nancy, look at these," she called.

Nancy took the photographs Bess handed her. They were all of the same beautiful blond woman, dressed in different costumes—sometimes even men's clothing.

"Maybe she was an actress playing male parts," Nancy suggested.

"Here she is with a cute little white dog," Bess went on, handing the pictures to Nancy. "And here she's with a Chinese man."

Nancy studied the photo carefully. "Isn't that the entry hall staircase she's standing on, with all those people?"

"You're right," George agreed, looking over Nancy's shoulder. "Maybe she was the owner of this place when it was a hotel. All these other people in the photo could have been her employees."

Abby had moved to the settee with another pile of old papers. "This is just what I need!" she called out. "These are scripts for old melodramas and songs, too. And look at this playbill!"

The girls crowded around Abby. The playbill advertised a play called *The Bandit's Treasure* at a hotel and saloon called the Golden Gardenia.

"*The Bandit's Treasure?*" Bess said. "That's Lizzie Applegate's play!"

Abby looked at Bess. "Lizzie Applegate?"

"She was a famous actress," Bess explained. "I read about her at that exhibit at the Land's End

Inn." Then she snapped her fingers. "That's it! I knew this blond woman looked familiar. Nancy, George—doesn't she look like Lizzie Applegate?" She held up one of the photos.

"There *is* a resemblance," George said.

"If this woman is Lizzie," Bess went on, "then this was probably Lizzie's hotel!"

"The exhibit said she owned a hotel after she retired from the theater," Nancy remembered. "But it said that the hotel burned."

Just then the doorbell rang. Rose got up to answer it. "What a beautiful tree!" they heard Rose exclaim from the entry hall. Nancy and the others turned to see Louis walk into the parlor, a huge Christmas tree balanced on his shoulder.

"When I purchased a tree for my store, I thought of you, Rose," he said, setting the tree down.

"Oh, how thoughtful, Louis." Rose gave Louis a quick peck on the cheek. "And, oh, wait until you see what we found!"

Louis's eyes gleamed when he saw the small green writing desk. He began to examine it with a professional eye, stroking the leather lid and pulling out drawers. "This *is* quite a discovery, Rose."

"And see what was inside!" Rose said.

Louis knelt down to look at the historical materials, his face becoming still and serious. He moved from one stack of paper to another, his eyes scouring the old documents.

"Let's take these photos to that table in the

second parlor," Bess suggested to Nancy and George. "We could put them together in a photo display for the entry hall. Abby, didn't you say that a lot of bed-and-breakfasts have historical displays in their lobbies?"

"A photo display in the entry would be great," Abby agreed, looking up from her scripts.

"We think the blond woman in the photographs might be Lizzie Applegate," Bess said to Louis.

Louis looked up from the papers he was examining. "Lizzie Apple— Uh, who? Who's that?" he asked.

"We saw an exhibit at the Land's End Inn about her," Bess explained again. "She was a famous actress in the late 1800s. After Lizzie retired from the theater, she opened a hotel. We think this house might be it! There's only one problem, though—Lizzie's hotel supposedly burned down."

Louis smiled at Bess. "Fascinating. Rose, I think you've found your historian."

"Tomorrow we're going to begin researching the house at the public library," Bess added.

"Yes, so you mentioned," Louis said, looking back at the photographs. "Well, this will make a charming lobby display. But of course, you have to complete the renovation first. As you know, time is running out."

Nancy thought she saw Rose flinch as Louis reminded them of their situation.

Just then Abby broke out singing. Holding one

of the song sheets from the desk, she sang to the tune of "Oh, Susanna!":

"I'll wait for you by the Golden Gate
   and hold your treasure true,
Where the rainbow ends in Christmas gold
   and the phoenix rises, too.
Oh, my love,
Ride far and fast for me.
I'll wait in Yerba Buena town,
In a house high above the sea."

"Oh, how romantic!" Bess exclaimed, clapping her hands.

"I have a book of old California songs downstairs on the piano, with a history of each song included," Abby said. "This song may be in it."

"I'll go get it!" cried Bess, dashing out.

"Be careful on the stairs," Abby called. "There isn't a light."

Turning her head, Nancy noticed a spark fly from the fire. "Watch out!" she said, swiftly stamping out the spark. "George, you'd better keep an eye on your fire. We really should have a fire screen."

Rose nodded. "You're right, Nancy. Abby, before we use the fireplace again, let's get a screen. We don't need any more accidents."

Abby nodded, still wrapped up in the play scripts. "I bought some fire extinguishers yesterday. There's one in the hall, one in the pantry, and another upstairs," she said.

Suddenly Nancy heard a bang, like a door slamming, then running footsteps. Startled, she looked up to see Bess in the doorway, her chest heaving and her eyes wide with fright.

"I saw her," Bess said in a whisper. She swallowed hard. "I saw Lizzie. Lizzie's ghost!"

6

The Ghost in the Mirror

"Hurry!" Bess cried. She ran from the parlor doorway to the back stairs. Nancy and George exchanged worried looks, then took off after Bess, followed by the others.

Nancy found her way down the dark stairs to the saloon. Bess pointed wildly at the huge mirror behind the bar. "There, in the mirror—I saw Lizzie!"

By now the others were in the saloon, too. "I'm sure it was just your imagination, dear," Rose said kindly.

"You've been staring at those photographs for hours," Abby added. "Your mind's playing tricks."

"No! I saw Lizzie!" Bess insisted.

"Tell us exactly what you saw," Nancy said. She knew her friend had an active imagination, but Bess would never make up a story. If Bess said she saw something, Nancy believed her.

"The ghost had blond hair in curls, and she was wearing men's clothing," Bess told Nancy. "I only saw her for a second, but I know that's what I saw."

"Perhaps you simply saw your own reflection," Louis suggested. "You have blond hair."

"Why, yes," Hannah added. "And you're wearing jeans—that would make your reflection look like it was wearing men's clothes."

Bess shook her head, her mouth drawn in a tight line. "I saw Lizzie!"

It was obvious to Nancy that Bess was upset. Just as on the night before, when the sink flooded, she felt frustrated that people didn't believe her. Nancy wrapped an arm around her friend, and George stood close beside her. "Don't worry. We'll find out what you saw," Nancy said.

Bess sighed. "Thanks, Nan." She walked over to the piano and grabbed the song book. "Might as well get what I came for," she muttered. Everyone filed upstairs.

Back in the parlor, Bess and Abby looked through the songbook. "Too bad," Abby said, shaking her head. "Lizzie's song isn't here."

Louis soon said good night and left. Hannah, Abby, and the girls decided it was time to go to bed. "I'll just stay up and finish hemming this curtain," said Rose, still at her sewing machine. "I'll keep an eye on the fire to make sure it's out before I come up."

*　*　*

51

The next afternoon Nancy sat in the periodicals room of the San Francisco public library. Pressing her forehead against the viewer on a microfilm projector, Nancy watched a series of old insurance maps whiz by on the film strip. The maps— the librarian had called them Sanborn maps— showed each building on every lot in old San Francisco.

With a crank on the side of the projector, she turned the microfilm reel to zero in on the map that included the block of California Street where the mansion stood. Neatly lettered on the map at the mansion's site was *The Golden Gardenia, hotel.*

So Rose and Abby's house *was* the same hotel as shown on the old playbills! Nancy smiled triumphantly. This historical research was fun.

Next, Nancy moved over to a shelf of old telephone directories, thick volumes bound in maroon leather. She took down the directory for 1894 and looked up the Golden Gardenia hotel. Running her finger down a column, she found its address on California Street—the same address as Rose and Abby's house.

Then she flipped through the pages until she found a listing for an E. Valdez. It was the same address!

But who was E. Valdez? Nancy mused. Abby had told them that the 1894 block book showed that same name as the owner of the lot where Rose and Abby's house stood. Just to make sure,

Nancy had double-checked the block book this afternoon. It had said E. Valdez all right.

E. Valdez. Could the *E* stand for Elizabeth, someone who might be nicknamed Lizzie? But why not Applegate? Why Valdez?

Nancy went back down the hall to the history room, where she had left Bess poring over old journals. "I've found out all sorts of stuff about Lizzie Applegate," Bess whispered eagerly.

"Good," Nancy said, checking her watch. "I found out some interesting stuff, too. But we're supposed to meet Hannah, Emily, and George at the Grand Hotel at four-thirty, and it's four-fifteen now. We can fill each other in over tea."

Outside, Nancy and Bess wrapped their coats tightly around them and headed for New Montgomery Street. George was waiting on the steps of the Grand Hotel. "Did you find the water department all right?" Nancy asked her. George's research task today had been to go to the water department on Mason Street to look up the original application for water at the mansion's site.

George nodded. "Mission accomplished."

"Nancy! Girls!" Nancy turned to see Hannah and Emily Foxworth hurrying up the sidewalk toward the hotel. Emily looked just as Nancy remembered her: a trim, energetic older woman with several cameras slung over her shoulder. Emily wore dark slacks, walking shoes, a close-fitting jacket, and a small brimmed hat.

Chattering merrily, the party entered the elegant old hotel. Emily led them to the Queen's Court, an enormous glass-domed room full of crystal chandeliers, potted palms, and marble columns. A waiter in a brocade vest led them to a low table surrounded by upholstered chairs and a small couch.

Nancy ordered camomile tea; Bess and George, blackcurrant tea; and Emily and Hannah, Earl Grey tea. They also asked the waiter to bring them some sandwiches and pastries.

The girls exchanged news with Emily. "Working on the restoration of that house must be fascinating," said Emily.

"Well, it certainly makes my muscles ache," Bess declared, rubbing her shoulder ruefully. "I was hanging wallpaper all day yesterday and all this morning. I've got glue caked all around my fingernails—yuck!"

The others chuckled. Then Nancy explained to Emily about their research project. She told the others what she had learned that day from the block books, the insurance maps, and the telephone directory.

The waiter brought their order, and everyone hungrily attacked the platter of food. "So tell us, George," Nancy said, "did you find the water application?"

George nodded. "Everything I found out supports what you learned," she reported. "The first application for water at the site was for the Golden Gardenia, a hotel. The application was dated 1888 and was signed by E. Valdez. A later application, dated 1906, was signed by Rachel Armstrong. It listed the building as a private residence."

Nancy nodded. "Rose said that the Armstrong sisters owned the house for years."

"Nancy, let me tell what I found out," Bess said, reaching for a cucumber sandwich. "Remember how Lizzie Applegate was an entertainer in the California gold mining camps and then a famous bandit, El Diablo, fell in love with her?"

"El Diablo?" said Emily. "In Spanish, that would mean 'The Devil.'"

Bess tossed her head. "He may have been a little devilish, but he was definitely romantic!" She sighed. "At the end of each of Lizzie's performances, he would ride a beautiful black horse up to the stage and leave her flowers. Then he would ride away before anyone could catch him. And get this—he usually left her gardenias."

"Wow! So if the hotel belonged to her, that would explain the name the Golden Gardenia," Nancy said.

Bess went on breathlessly. "Each time he came, the bandit would appear suddenly and then disappear. One day Lizzie and the bandit rode away together on his beautiful horse!" Excited, Bess leaned forward, her uneaten sandwich in her hand. "People thought Lizzie had joined the bandit's gang. Then on Christmas Day in 1878, there was a big stagecoach robbery."

"The bandit?" Nancy asked.

Bess nodded, her eyes glowing. "Right after that, the bandit and his gang were ambushed. But the bandit escaped, and a woman with long blond curls was seen riding away with him!"

"Lizzie?" Hannah asked with a smile.

"It has to be!" said Bess. "Anyway, Lizzie came to San Francisco right after that and began acting in melodramas at the Bella Union Theater. She became a famous actress. That's when she wrote *The Bandit's Treasure*. And then she opened a big hotel. But the hotel burned down only a year later," she finished, biting mournfully into her sandwich.

"The history books must have it wrong. The Golden Gardenia didn't burn down," Hannah said. "At least, it was still there this morning!" Everyone laughed.

"Wait, I'm confused," said Emily, looking over the rim of her teacup. "All the records show that the hotel on California Street—the Golden Gardenia, right?—was owned by an E. Valdez. So why do you think it's Lizzie Applegate's hotel?"

"That's part of what we're trying to figure out," Nancy explained. "The playbills we found said that Lizzie's play, *The Bandit's Treasure*, was being performed at the Golden Gardenia. And the pictures we found showed a woman who looked just like Lizzie, posing with her staff on the staircase of Rose and Abby's house."

"I just know the Golden Gardenia was Lizzie's hotel," Bess insisted.

"Did you ever find out El Diablo's real name?" Emily asked.

"No," Bess admitted. "But Valdez is a Spanish name, isn't it? And El Diablo is Spanish."

"I think we're all thinking the same thing," Nancy said. "Maybe E. Valdez was Lizzie's married name—after she married the bandit."

"Why don't you girls visit the California Express Company museum?" Emily said. "I did some research there when I was illustrating an article on treasure hunters. I'll bet the bandit robbed some of their stagecoaches. Maybe the museum historians would know his real name. That might answer the Valdez question."

"Good idea," Nancy said. "Thanks, Emily."

Bess suddenly dug into her purse. "Speaking of questions," she said to Emily, "I have one for you." She showed Emily the photograph she'd taken of Rose, Abby, Hannah, Nancy, and George their first night in San Francisco. Pointing out the white mist overhead, she asked, "Could that be a ghost?"

Emily laughed. "You have quite an imagination, Bess," she said. "More likely, it's a distortion from reflected light. Or even a blemish on the film."

Disappointed, Bess put the photograph away.

After they finished their tea, Hannah and Emily left to do some window shopping before going to a play that night. The girls caught a bus back to the mansion.

"I hope Rose and Abby found some good

bargains at that estate sale this afternoon," George said as they walked back to the mansion from the bus stop. "Rose said that all the furnishings of one big house were being sold after the owner died. I guess Rose and Abby still need a lot of furniture for all the guest rooms."

"Yes, and they want all antiques to make the house look really authentic," Bess added. "At least, Rose does. But I heard Abby this morning telling Rose they couldn't afford so many antiques and they should just buy new stuff. I think that would be such a shame."

Nancy glanced ahead toward the house. As she looked, a figure came racing down the sidewalk toward them. Nancy realized it was the same blond teenager she had seen before, the one who had waved through the restaurant window at Mary Lee.

As he came closer, Nancy saw that he was holding a large bundle under his ragged army coat. His face was pale, and his eyes were wild with panic.

"Hey!" Nancy yelled as he charged at them. But the boy didn't stop. He darted around the girls and ran on down the street.

"What in the—" Bess began.

But she didn't get a chance to finish. Nancy grabbed Bess's arm, pointing with her other hand toward Rose and Abby's house.

A trail of black smoke was pouring out of one of the windows in the front parlor!

7

Evidence in the Ashes

"The mansion's on fire!" Nancy shouted.

The girls raced down the sidewalk. They heard sirens wailing in the distance, and just as they reached the burning building, two fire trucks roared up.

Jumping off the truck, the firefighters grabbed their hoses and headed for the house. Just then the girls saw Louis Chandler come rushing out the front door with a fire extinguisher. "Anyone else inside?" a firefighter stopped to ask Louis.

"No. No one's home," Louis panted, his face and clothes covered with soot. "I tried to put out the fire, but I couldn't."

Suddenly Abby appeared at the front door in her bathrobe, clutching her cat Alfreida in her arms. She looked around helplessly, her face a mixture of fright and confusion. Nancy ran up the steps to help guide Abby down to the sidewalk. A firefighter yelled to the crew to check the house for other occupants.

Louis stared at Abby in surprise. "Abby! I thought you and Rose went to the estate sale."

"I felt sick, so I stayed home," Abby said, her voice quavering. "I just woke up, and I heard the sirens. What's going on?"

Louis mopped his brow. "A fire!"

Abby looked stunned. "Oh, no," she whispered. "But how . . ." Her voice trailed off as she looked up at the mansion in dismay.

"Thank goodness you woke up," Bess said. "Louis didn't know you were here when he tried to put the fire out."

Abby turned to Louis. "You were here?"

"I was walking past the house," Louis said, "when I smelled smoke. The door was unlocked, so I ran in and tried to put out the fire."

"The front door was unlocked?" Abby repeated, dazed. Nancy frowned, wondering the same thing.

"Where's Charlie?" Louis asked.

"He left at about four," Abby said. "He went to the lumber yard to buy roofing supplies so he could repair the tower roof."

A crowd had begun to gather across the street. Nancy scanned the faces, but she didn't see the blond boy. He had been coming from the direction of the fire when she saw him. Who is he? she wondered, frowning. And what does he know about the fire?

The firefighters quickly extinguished the blaze. A firefighter in a white helmet came out the door and introduced himself to Louis, Abby, and the girls as Chief Martinez.

"Any idea how the fire started?" Louis asked.

Chief Martinez rubbed his jaw. "We're investigating that right now. But that fire in the fireplace may be the source. You have no fire screen. People have no business starting a fire without a protective screen."

Abby grew pale and held Alfreida close. "Rose told me not to," she said in a shaky voice, "but I was cold. And I was watching the fire, I really was! But then, about four-thirty, I felt sick to my stomach, so I put it out and went upstairs to read in bed. I was *sure* I put the fire out."

Nancy watched Abby closely. She certainly seemed to be telling the truth.

Chief Martinez spoke sternly. "You need a screen, ma'am. A fire can look like it's out, but one spark can make it flare up again. And these old houses can go up in minutes. Fortunately, this fire didn't do much damage, thanks to your friend here. He got here just in time. It looks like you had a lot of paper spread out on the carpet, though—that went up like tinder."

Abby's lower lip twitched. She looked close to tears. "The historical documents," she groaned. Nancy, George, and Bess looked at each other in dismay.

The fire chief turned to Louis. "And next time, sir, don't try to put out the fire yourself," he said. "You could have been injured. You were the one who called the fire department?"

Louis shook his head. "No."

The chief shrugged. "Well, somebody did. Maybe one of your neighbors saw the smoke."

Abby was still staring dully at the house. "Another accident," she murmured.

Nancy's eyes traveled from Abby's stricken face to the mansion. She had the uneasy feeling that the fire was not just "another accident."

Chief Martinez left to confer with his squad. Then a police car pulled up and a plainclothes detective stepped out. Nancy's eyes lit up. "Lieutenant Chin!" she called. Nancy and George had met Lieutenant Donald Chin while working on Emily Foxworth's case. They ran over to him.

"Nancy Drew! And George, too!" Lieutenant Chin looked surprised. "What are you doing here?"

"We're out here helping some friends renovate this house," Nancy told him. "A fire broke out in the parlor while we were gone this afternoon."

Chin nodded. "I heard the sirens and decided to stop by."

Nancy glanced around to make sure no one else was listening. "Well, Lieutenant, maybe you should know that there have been a series of 'accidents' in this house lately," she told him quietly.

"You're suggesting the fire was deliberate?" Lieutenant Chin asked with an attentive glance.

Nancy hesitated. "I have no evidence. Yet."

He nodded. "I'll take a look around inside," he

said. "And if you find something or if I can help in any way, call me."

Nancy accepted the card Lieutenant Chin pulled from his pocket and shook his hand. "As soon as I have evidence, I *will* call you."

"Do that. And please give my best to Emily when you see her." He excused himself and went to talk with Chief Martinez.

The firefighters cleaned up their equipment and piled back into the trucks. Abby, Louis, and the girls were given the all-clear to go back inside. As Lieutenant Chin came back outside, he threw Nancy a baffled look that told her he'd found no evidence.

Abby headed straight for the parlor to survey the damage, with Louis and the girls close behind. The carpet in front of the fireplace was drenched with water from the fire hoses. The wallpaper on the fireplace wall was black with smoke, but the rest of the furnishings had not burned. The historical documents, though, were now a mass of wet black ashes.

"At least I have the manuscript for *The Bandit's Treasure*," Abby said sadly. "I took that upstairs to read."

"And the photos didn't burn," Bess added, moving into the back parlor to examine the old photographs she had laid out on the table there.

Abby looked at Louis gratefully. "I'd hate to think what might have happened if you hadn't gotten here," she said.

From the window, Nancy saw Charlie drive up, the bed of his truck loaded with building supplies. She went outside to meet him. As she told him about the fire, she watched his reaction carefully.

"What?" Charlie croaked. The wrinkles around his eyes deepened as he scrutinized the house. "How much damage?" he asked wearily.

"Mostly some historical papers we were looking at last night," Nancy said. "And the wallpaper and carpeting by the fireplace."

Charlie shook his head. "I wasn't gone very long," he said in a dull, desperate tone of voice. "When will it end?" He limped slowly back to his truck to unload the supplies.

Nancy bit her lip. Her instincts told her that he had known nothing about the fire. But how could she be sure? An idea hit her. "Can I help you unload that stuff?" she offered.

Charlie looked surprised. "Uh, okay. Thanks."

Nancy hurried to his pickup truck and reached for a sack. When Charlie turned away, she peeked in the bag, saw a sales slip, and pulled it out.

At the top of the sales slip was printed a store's address, out in Oakland—an hour's drive away. And the time of the sale was printed on the slip: 5:13 P.M. Abby had said she was still in the parlor at 4:30. Charlie would have had to leave the house well before then to be at the store and make his purchase at 5:13. He couldn't have started the fire!

Nancy helped him carry his supplies inside and then returned to the front parlor. Only George and Bess were there, scooping up the wet, charred paper and dumping it in a large trash can. "Be careful," Nancy said as she knelt down to help them. "We need to save the paper. If this is a case of arson, the police will need evidence."

Nancy tugged gently at a sodden clump of black paper. Reaching for a loose piece, she stopped suddenly and stared at the paper's top right corner. The corner had escaped the flames somehow, and some handwriting was still visible on it. It was a date—1982.

Nancy stared in disbelief. All the papers they had been looking at the night before were dated from the 1800s!

Louis entered the parlor and noticed Nancy staring at the paper. "What is it?" he asked.

Nancy looked up quickly. "Oh, nothing," she said, shrugging. But as she bent back to her cleanup work, she slipped the scrap of paper into her skirt pocket.

Louis and George moved the furniture into the second parlor, and Nancy and Bess started to roll up the wet, burned carpet. They heard a car pull up outside, and a minute later Rose burst through the door of the parlor. She gasped, then stood frozen, staring at the blackened fireplace wall.

Louis put his arm sympathetically around Rose's tiny figure and led her out to the kitchen. "At least we have fire insurance," Nancy heard Rose telling Louis in a brave but shaky voice. "Abby insisted on it."

"Poor Rose," Bess murmured. "I don't know how much more she can take."

Nancy nodded grimly, but she thought to herself, Why had Abby insisted on fire insurance?

A half hour later the cleanup was more or less finished. Abby, saying she wasn't feeling well, went to bed early. Louis took Rose out to dinner. The girls decided to go back to the Chinese restaurant.

When they walked in, they saw Mary Lee sitting with a large family group around one of the big round tables. She waved and jumped up. "We saw the fire trucks," she said anxiously. "Is everything all right?"

"We had a scare," Nancy admitted, "but fortunately the fire damage was minor."

"Thank goodness," Mary said. "Come on and join our family. It's a slow night, so we're eating together."

Mary helped them pull up chairs and introduced them to her family: her father and mother, her grandmother and grandfather, her uncle Ray and aunt June, her brother Sam, and her cousins Winston and Lorraine. Mary explained to the Lees that the girls were helping to restore the Victorian mansion down the street.

Mary's grandfather looked excited. "My father worked there when it was a hotel," he said. "He was the cook."

The girls exchanged glances. Maybe Mary's grandfather could tell them more about Lizzie. "When was that?" Nancy asked.

"Up until 1906, the year of the earthquake," the grandfather answered. "When the owner died, the hotel closed. Then my father opened a restaurant in Chinatown. It's still there. My son Ray is the manager." He pointed to Mary's uncle. "We opened our second restaurant, here, two years ago."

Nancy knit her eyebrows. "Mr. Lee," she said, "we found a photograph of a Chinese man standing with a woman who we think was the owner of the hotel. Maybe that man is your father."

Bess perked up, eyes sparkling. "Hang on, I'll go get it!" She dashed from the restaurant.

When Bess returned minutes later, Mary's grandfather examined the old photograph carefully. He broke into a smile. "Yes, this is my father," he said. "And I recognize this woman from my father's photographs. She was the hotel's owner." Mr. Lee passed the photo around the table.

Nancy's heart beat hard with excitement. "Do you know the name of the hotel's owner?" she asked.

"Lizzie," Mr. Lee answered at once.

"And her last name?" Nancy prodded.

"I never knew her last name," Mr. Lee said. "My father only called her Lizzie."

It was quite late when the party broke up. Nancy, George, and Bess thanked Mary and her parents, then Mary walked the girls to the door.

At the door, Nancy turned to Mary. "There's something I wanted to ask," she said. "I saw a guy with blond hair running down the street today just before the fire trucks arrived. I've seen him before, outside your restaurant and in the neighborhood. Who is he? Do you know him?"

Mary looked over her shoulder, avoiding Nancy's eyes. "Uh, well . . ." Mary mumbled. Just then the door to the restaurant opened and a young couple entered. Looking relieved, Mary excused herself to show the couple to a table.

Outside, Nancy wondered at Mary's strange response. She was sure now that Mary knew the boy. But why didn't she want to admit that to Nancy?

The girls hurried through the cold night air back to the mansion. Inside, the smell of smoke was still strong. They tiptoed upstairs.

"It's freezing!" Bess said. "I can't wait to get into bed."

"Good luck trying to fall asleep," George said. "That smoky smell is giving me a headache."

Nancy turned from the bureau and paused to smell the air. The smoky smell was certainly there, but there seemed to be something else.

"What is it, Nan?" George said.

Nancy shook her head. "I guess it's nothing." She reached to the headboard, pulling back the quilt. Then she gave a start.

Bess and George ran over. "What?" Bess cried. Nancy pointed to the pillow.

Lying on the white pillowcase was a small piece of notepaper. A single line was typed across it: "Leave the mansion at once!"

8

A Fragrant Message

Bess gasped. " 'Leave the mansion!' Why? Who can be threatening us?"

Nancy picked up the note. Her nose wrinkled as she sniffed the notepaper. "That's what I was smelling," she said. "This paper."

George sniffed the paper. "Some kind of flowery perfume," she said, making a disgusted face.

Bess leaned over to take a whiff, and Nancy took another one. Then they looked up at each other. "Gardenia," they said at the same time.

"Gardenia?" George said.

Nancy nodded. "They have a very distinctive fragrance," she said.

"And gardenias are the kind of flowers El Diablo brought Lizzie," Bess said excitedly. "Maybe the note is from Lizzie—from Lizzie's ghost!"

"There are no ghosts, Bess," George declared.

Bess plopped on the bed. "Then who left the note?"

"Whoever started the fire," Nancy guessed.

George eyed Nancy carefully. "Do you think the fire was just another fake accident?"

"Yes," Nancy answered. She pulled the half-burned scrap of paper from her pocket. "I found this in the mess in the parlor."

George studied the paper. "Nineteen eighty-two?"

Bess looked confused. "But the papers in the desk all dated from the 1800s. This date has to be wrong."

"Exactly," Nancy said.

"Maybe another letter got mixed up with the old papers," Bess suggested. "Rose said she'd been going through her correspondence, remember? Maybe one of her old letters accidentally fell into the pile of historical stuff."

"Good thinking," Nancy said. "We'll ask Rose if any of her letters is missing. But if this *is* one of Rose's letters, maybe it wasn't so accidental. Just think—how do we know it was the historical documents that got burned? All we could see was a bunch of charred paper."

"I don't get it," George said. "We left the papers in front of the fireplace. If they didn't burn, where are they?"

"Exactly," Nancy said. "I think somebody may have stolen Lizzie's papers. And to cover up the theft, the thief put other papers—such as Rose's letters—in their place. Then he or she burned the substitute letters, so we'd think the real ones were lost in the fire."

Bess jumped up from the bed. "There *is* a secret in Lizzie's papers! I knew it! That's why someone stole them!"

"Do you think the same person who stole the letters and started the fire caused the other accidents, too?" George asked.

Nancy nodded. "Someone wants to learn Lizzie's secret. And I bet that same person is trying to keep the mansion from opening as a hotel. But I don't know why," she added almost to herself.

"Who are your suspects?" Bess asked.

Nancy frowned. "Abby was home when the fire started," she pointed out.

"Abby wouldn't vandalize her own property," Bess protested. "Besides, she was sleeping upstairs."

"She *said* she was sleeping," George corrected Bess. "Maybe Abby thinks there's a clue to the house's secret in Lizzie's papers, and she wants to keep it to herself?"

Nancy looked thoughtful. "I heard Rose tell Louis that Abby insisted on fire insurance," she recalled. "Maybe Abby wants out of this bed-and-breakfast business, but Rose won't quit. So Abby starts a fire, the mansion burns, and she files an insurance claim. And Abby gets out of the hotel project without losing any money."

"But besides Abby, who are your suspects?" Bess asked Nancy, eager to know more.

"Charlie has an alibi," Nancy said. "He was at the building supply store. I saw a sales slip in one

71

of his bags that definitely proves he couldn't have been here when the fire was started. Of course, that still doesn't clear him of the other incidents."

"Anybody else?" George asked.

"Well, there's that blond kid we saw running down the street before the fire," Nancy answered. "Who is he, and why is he always hanging around here? Mary was awfully evasive when I asked her about him. I think she's hiding something."

"But how could the kid have gotten inside to start the fire?" George pointed out.

"Louis said he found the door unlocked," Nancy reminded her.

"What about the note, Nancy?" Bess asked. "Who could have left that?"

"Abby and Charlie were both here when we left tonight," Nancy noted. "And who knows? Maybe the blond boy sneaked into the house somehow."

Bess sighed. "Almost everybody's a suspect," she said. "Where can we start?"

"First thing tomorrow, we ask Rose if any of her letters are missing," Nancy said. "If they are, that might mean someone made a switch."

"And then?" asked George.

"Then we search for Lizzie's papers," Nancy replied. "And the first place I'd like to search is Abby's room."

* * *

The next morning Nancy hurried downstairs to the kitchen. Hannah was there, dressed for work in jeans and an old T-shirt, her hair pulled back in a bandanna. She was reading the newspaper and eating a bowl of oatmeal.

"Morning, Hannah. Where's Rose?" Nancy asked.

"Rose and Louis went to an auction early this morning," Hannah said. "They're hoping to find a chandelier for the entry."

Nancy sat at the kitchen table. "What happened to the drawer?" she asked, pointing to a drawer of utensils sitting on the table.

"It's broken," Hannah said, putting down the paper. "I tried to fix it myself, but I couldn't. Maybe Charlie can look at it today."

Nancy put some English muffins in the toaster and poured herself some juice. Soon George and Bess ambled into the kitchen. "You guys are up early," Hannah commented.

"We thought we'd get an early start so that we can visit the California Express Company this afternoon, like Emily suggested," Bess explained, reaching for the coffeepot. "What's the work schedule for today?"

"You and I are stripping wallpaper again." Hannah sighed and got up from the table.

"Not more wallpaper!" Bess groaned.

"Would you rather be outside chipping paint with Nancy and me?" George teased.

"Uh, no thanks," Bess said hastily.

"Is Abby up yet, Hannah?" Nancy asked.

"No, she says she's still sick," Hannah said. "She asked me to call her if she didn't come down by one o'clock. The insurance agent's coming this afternoon to make an inspection of the fire scene. I hope nothing serious is wrong with Abby," she added, looking concerned.

Nancy nodded and murmured sympathetically. She, too, hoped Abby wasn't seriously ill. But on the other hand, she was impatient to check Abby's room. And if Abby *wasn't* sick, Nancy thought, she was acting awfully strange.

"I never knew stagecoaches were so huge!" Bess exclaimed, eyeing an old coach.

George read the sign beside the coach. "This says as many as eighteen people traveled on a stagecoach—nine inside, nine on top," she said.

Nancy smiled. "So the coach probably didn't seem so big after all," she remarked.

The girls stood in the lobby of the California Express Company museum, looking at the displays while waiting for a historian to help them. Bess peered into a case displaying tiny mounds of gold dust from different regions. "This is real gold! Isn't it beautiful!"

"Nancy Drew?" A young woman in her midtwenties appeared behind them. She introduced herself as Lisa Morley, one of the staff historians. "The receptionist told me you were interested in doing some research," she said.

"Yes," Nancy said. "We're particularly interested in a stagecoach robber who went by the name of El Diablo."

"We have lots of information on El Diablo," Lisa said, leading the girls up a flight of stairs. "Is there anything in particular you're looking for?"

"Do you know his real name?" asked Nancy eagerly.

"Why, yes—Diego Valdez," Lisa responded.

The girls broke into smiles.

"Were Diego and Lizzie Applegate married?" Bess asked as they walked into a research office upstairs. "Was Lizzie also Elizabeth Valdez?"

"I've never seen proof of their marriage," Lisa answered. "But it wouldn't surprise me. They were certainly in love with each other."

"Did Lizzie's hotel burn down?" George asked.

"Her first hotel, on Ellis Street, burned," Lisa said.

"Her first one? Then there was more than one?" Nancy asked.

"Oh, yes," Lisa said. She perched on the edge of a table, clearly enjoying her subject. "After she retired from the theater, Lizzie opened a magnificent hotel downtown. That was the one that burned, and unfortunately for history, most of her papers burned up then, too. Several years later, though, she opened another hotel farther out."

"Where was it?" Nancy pumped her.

Lisa shrugged. "We don't know," she admitted. "The address under which it was originally registered happened to be wrong—these things happen. But that mistake has made it hard to trace the real building. And Lizzie's fame was fading by then, so the second hotel wasn't as well known as the first."

"What was the second hotel's name?" Bess asked.

"It was called the Golden Gardenia," Lisa said, "just as the first hotel was."

Nancy drew a deep breath. "We believe we're staying in Lizzie's second hotel," she told Lisa. "It's a run-down Victorian that we're helping to renovate on California Street." She proceeded to tell Lisa about their discoveries.

Lisa was excited to hear about the old papers they'd found but dismayed to hear about the fire. Nancy thought it best not to raise the historian's hopes with the idea that the historical papers might still exist.

"But these didn't burn," Bess said, pulling out the old photos they had found. She showed Lisa the picture of the blond woman in men's clothing. "Did Lizzie ever dress like a man?" Bess asked.

"She did," Lisa said, smiling at the photo. "I imagine Lizzie liked the freedom men's clothing gave her. Even out West, women had a restricted life during the 1800s. A man could go anywhere and do almost anything. A woman couldn't."

The girls bombarded the historian with questions as they flipped through the photos.

"Lizzie had a diverse life," Lisa told them. "For example, as she grew older, she was famous for holding séances. Most people thought the séances were just a publicity stunt. But others thought she was trying to contact El Diablo."

"Then he was dead?" Nancy asked.

"We can't be sure," Lisa said. "But he was never seen after his last robbery, on Christmas Day in 1878. He and his gang robbed a stagecoach of a big shipment of gold, but they were ambushed by a posse of detectives soon after the robbery. The detectives wounded El Diablo, but they didn't kill him. He disappeared with the gold."

"How romantic!" Bess sighed.

"Some said he escaped to Mexico with the gold," Lisa went on. "Others said he left the money with Lizzie. Maybe he came back and got it, maybe he didn't. It was sixty thousand dollars in 1878 gold coins. With that much money at stake, there were bound to be a lot of wild stories."

Nancy nodded. "I can imagine!"

After thanking Lisa for her help, the girls left the museum and took a bus back to the mansion, talking excitedly about what they'd learned.

Back at the house, Nancy slid her key in the warped front door and pushed hard. She saw at once a spectacular chandelier hanging in the entry. A hundred crystal pendants showered the entry hall with sparkling light.

"Rose and Louis found the chandelier they were looking for," Nancy said, awed.

"It's beautiful," Bess agreed, stepping inside behind Nancy.

The last to come in, George turned to slam shut the warped door. Then she, too, looked up. The crystal chandelier seemed to dance through the air.

Then, as if on cue, the huge ornate lighting fixture came crashing to the floor!

9

Time Is Running Out

Nancy grabbed Bess's arm, pulling her out of the way.

"Aaah!" Bess's cry rang out as the broken chandelier fell with a crash on the entry hall floor.

Nancy heard a gasp and saw the mirrored door to the parlor open. Abby stood in the doorway, looking at the chandelier remnants in astonishment. "I—I saw what happened," she said shakily, "through the two-way mirror."

"George, are you all right?" Nancy said.

George nodded, checking her pant legs. "I don't think any pieces hit me. I can still go running with Mary later."

Rose and Hannah rushed in from the back hall, followed by Charlie, a screwdriver in his hand. They all stopped and stared wide-eyed at the fallen chandelier.

Rose opened her mouth to speak, but Abby cut her off. "How can we open the hotel?" she burst out, almost hysterically. "Rose, don't you see? We just hung that chandelier, and now it crashes down. The accidents don't stop! This house is cursed!"

Nancy stepped gingerly into the pile of crystal shards, bending over to survey the debris. Amidst the shattered glass, she spied a broken link from the chandelier's brass chain. She quickly pocketed it.

As Nancy looked up, Rose was gazing at the broken glass, tears brimming in her eyes. But as Rose turned to Abby, her voice was firm. "I won't give up, Abby," she said. "Now, let's get this mess cleaned up."

Within a few minutes they had swept the floor and scooped all the jagged pieces into a box. Charlie carted it off to the garbage.

Upstairs, in the Blue Room, Nancy showed her friends the broken chain link. "Someone filed through the brass plating on the link, all the way down to the steel core," Nancy said. "When you slammed the front door, George, the vibrations probably started the chandelier swinging. The chain snapped."

"If the chain link was filed, then the chandelier breaking wasn't an accident," George said, fingering the piece of brass.

Nancy nodded. "Someone knew that that front door has to be slammed shut," she said. "The chandelier must have been rigged to fall at the slightest vibration."

"But who would do that?" Bess asked.

"Charlie?" George suggested.

"He's the most likely person to have a metal file," Nancy noted. "You'd need a tool like that to file through the metal chain."

"Abby was right on the scene," Bess pointed out.

George nodded. "She seemed very upset by the crash," she remarked, "but maybe that was just an act. She sure does sound ready to give up on the hotel. That could be why she'd be creating accidents to persuade Rose to sell."

Nancy sighed, looking at the metal link. "I don't know who's responsible," she said. "But I just know this is connected to the fire and all the other accidents. We have to keep on investigating, before someone gets hurt. I'm going to ask Rose right now if any of her letters are missing."

Nancy went to the bureau, opened the top drawer, and took out the charred piece of paper she had found after the fire. Then she went downstairs to find Rose.

Rose was standing in the entry hall, gazing at the stained-glass window over the front door. When she saw Nancy on the stairs, she gave a start.

"I'm sorry if I startled you, Rose," Nancy said, approaching her. "Do you have a minute?"

"Of course. What is it, Nancy?" Rose said.

"You said you had been going through your old letters. Where are they?" Nancy asked.

"Why, they're in the old rolltop desk in the office," Rose replied, surprised.

"Would you show me?" Nancy asked.

Rose led Nancy into her office, a small room off the entry hall. An antique rolltop desk nearly filled the tiny office. Rose lifted the lid of the desk. She paused, then began fingering the stacks of papers piled there. "I left them right here on top of the bills," she murmured, in confusion.

Nancy held out the scrap of burned paper. "Does this look familiar?"

Rose stared at the corner of burned paper. "Why, yes. That's my sister Margaret's handwriting." Then she gasped. "Oh, Nancy! You don't think my letters burned, too?"

"I'm sorry, Rose, but I do think so," Nancy said gently. "Who knew your letters were here?"

"Well, Abby does, of course. Charlie, too, I imagine," Rose added, thinking. "And Louis knew—he dropped by one night when I was working on my Christmas cards. But, Nancy, how could my letters have burned? The fire was in the parlor." Rose began frantically opening the drawers of the desk. "Maybe Abby put them away somewhere else. I'll ask her."

"No," Nancy said firmly. "Please don't say anything to anybody—not until we know who is responsible."

Rose looked pained. "Well . . . all right, Nancy. I won't. But please—find my letters!"

"I'll try," Nancy promised. But inside, she had a feeling that it was already too late.

* * *

After dinner that night—Rose served her special pot roast—Nancy, Bess, and George threw on their coats and strolled over to Sacramento Street, where Louis had said the vintage clothing stores were. The brightly lit shops were open late for holiday shopping. "The dresses we found in the trunk should be perfect for the Winter Festival," Bess chattered happily. "But we still need hats, shawls, gloves——"

"Hold on, Bess." George laughed. "How much were you planning to spend? Did you find El Diablo's treasure or something?"

Nancy smiled too, then grew thoughtful. "Speaking of El Diablo's treasure," she said, "let's not mention to anybody how much money the stolen gold would be worth. Sixty thousand dollars in 1878 gold coins would be worth a fortune today. I don't want to get Rose's hopes up."

"Oh, all right," Bess agreed with a sigh. "But it doesn't matter how much money it was—it's just such a cool story."

"Look, there's Louis's store," George said, pointing across the street. "Chandler Interiors. Should we stop in and say hello?"

Nancy turned to look at the shop, its front window full of old-fashioned Christmas toys. Then she did a double take. At the curb in front of Louis's store, a green-and-white taxi was parked—with Charlie at the wheel.

Nancy instinctively crouched behind a mailbox for cover. "What is it, Nan?" George asked.

Nancy pointed. "Look, in that cab!"

Nancy leaned over to get a better view. Bay City Cab, she read on the side of the taxi. A young blond woman was seated on the front seat beside Charlie, deep in a serious conversation with him. She was clearly not a paying passenger.

George looked and shrugged. "So? Charlie already told you he had a second job."

Just then the girl got out of the cab, walked up to Louis's store, and went inside. Nancy grabbed George's arm. "Come on, guys, let's visit Louis," Nancy said, eager to find out more.

When they entered the store, they saw the blond girl standing behind the counter. She was talking on the telephone and chewing a strand of her long hair. Trying to look casual, George and Bess stopped at a display case full of antique jewelry. Nancy spotted a beautiful armoire in the office at the rear of the shop and wandered back to look at it.

"That isn't part of the store!" a voice behind her called sharply. Nancy turned to see the blond girl hurrying toward her.

Nancy smiled. "I just noticed the armoire," she said. "That's why I came back. We're staying in the neighborhood," she added, hoping to start a conversation. "We're restoring a mansion over on California Street."

The girl seemed to relax. "Yeah? My dad's working on a house over there," she said. "His name is Charlie Webber. Do you know him?"

"Sure," Nancy said. Now it made sense why

the girl was sitting with Charlie in the front of the cab. But why was Charlie's daughter working in Louis's store?

"I'm Cassandra," the girl said. Nancy shook her hand and introduced herself.

Just then Louis walked into the shop. He glanced at Bess and George in surprise, then looked around sharply. He spotted Cassandra and Nancy in the office. With a guilty gulp, Cassandra hurried back to the front counter. Nancy joined Bess and George at the jewelry case.

"Welcome to Chandler Interiors, girls," Louis was saying to them. "See anything you like?"

Bess pointed at the jewelry. "I love the cameos," she said. "And that green brooch is really awesome."

Louis smiled. "Isn't it?" he said. "It's emerald. A fairly common piece from the last century, but it does have a certain charm."

Proud of his antiques, Louis showed the girls some fine porcelain and silver pieces, a carved desk with secret drawers, and a beautiful crystal chandelier. "Did you see the chandelier Rose and I found this morning?" he asked. "She loved it so much, I bought it on the spot. Charlie and Abby were going to clean it up and hang it."

The girls exchanged nervous looks. "I'm afraid there was another accident," Nancy told him. "The chandelier fell from its ceiling chain. It was completely shattered."

Louis's jaw dropped. "No!" he cried in dismay.

"Oh, it can't be! Rose loved it so much. And it was *such* an exquisite piece."

"Do you have any idea why there have been so many accidents at the mansion?" Nancy asked.

"Of course not," he declared. "If I did, I would stop them—at once." Then he grew thoughtful. "Renovations just shouldn't be this difficult. Perhaps it's as Rose says: The house is jinxed."

Nancy didn't agree, but she said nothing. The three girls thanked Louis and made their way back to California Street.

Rose was taking a cake out of the oven as they walked into the kitchen. The sounds of piano playing drifted up from the saloon. "You're just in time," she said as she placed the cake on top of the refrigerator to cool. "We decided this place needed a little Christmas spirit. Abby and Hannah are downstairs with some hot cider and fudge. We thought we'd do some singing and maybe string some popcorn for the Christmas tree. How about it?"

"Sounds great," Nancy said. The girls followed Rose downstairs, mugs of hot cider in hand. Everyone gathered around the piano as Abby began to play. At Bess's request, they started off by singing the song from *The Bandit's Treasure*.

As Nancy looked for a place to set down her cider mug, she spotted Charlie's tool kit in the corner. Instantly she thought of the filed-through chandelier chain. "Does Charlie have a metal file?" she asked as they paused between songs.

"The edge of my jacket zipper is jagged. I'd like to file it down."

"I know he does," Rose said. She turned to Abby. "Abby, didn't you borrow Charlie's file to fix that broken utensil drawer in the kitchen?"

"Yes, but I couldn't fix it so I put the file back in his tool kit," Abby said, looking up from the piano.

Nancy bent down to search Charlie's tool kit. "I don't see a metal file here," she reported.

"That's odd," Rose said. "Charlie is very particular about keeping his tools together."

"How did you meet Charlie, by the way?" Nancy asked casually as she returned to the piano.

"Through Louis," Rose replied. "Charlie has worked for some of Louis's clients before. Why do you ask, Nancy?"

"Just curious," Nancy answered. Then, looking up, she noticed Abby watching her closely. Nancy smiled brightly. "Another song, Abby?"

Abby abruptly turned back to the keyboard. Nancy joined the others in singing holiday songs, but she couldn't help feeling uneasy.

Later that night, after the girls went to bed, Nancy lay awake pondering the mansion's chain of accidents. She could hear Bess and George breathing deeply. Closing her eyes, she willed herself to forget the mystery and relax.

Suddenly a loud clatter came from downstairs. Nancy's eyes popped open. George and Bess sat bolt upright, awakened by the noise. Scrambling out of bed and grabbing their robes, the girls raced downstairs. Nancy went into the kitchen first, turning on the light.

Beside the refrigerator a kitchen chair lay tipped over on its side. George righted the chair while Nancy and Bess looked around the room.

"Hey!" George said in surprise.

Nancy and Bess turned around. George was standing on the chair, picking up the cake that Rose had put on the refrigerator to cool. As George stepped down, Nancy could see that a large piece of cake was missing. On the cake plate, coated with crumbs, lay a metal file.

Nancy stepped over and picked up the file. "This is probably what was used to cut the chandelier chain," she said. "What do you want to bet this is Charlie's missing file?"

"But how did it get here?" George asked.

"Abby was using it in the kitchen to fix the drawer," Nancy said. "But she says she put it back in the tool kit."

"Maybe she was sneaking a piece of cake," Bess suggested tentatively.

"Why would she use a metal file for that?" George said skeptically.

"Let's look around," Nancy suggested. The girls wandered through the kitchen and pantry, making sure all the windows and doors were locked. Then they stepped into the dining room. Suddenly Nancy pulled up short.

The curtains around the jib door fluttered in the night wind. The jib door was open!

10

Secret Words Remembered

Nancy rushed through the open jib door into the backyard. She squinted in the darkness but saw no one. Except for the noise of distant car traffic, all she could hear was the muffled sound of a dog barking.

Then her eye caught sight of something on the dirt path that cut through the garden. Her heart leapt—it was Abby's long fringed purple scarf! She picked it up and went back inside.

"Abby's scarf!" Bess exclaimed as Nancy stepped through the door. "So it *was* Abby trying to steal a piece of cake."

"If that's all it is, then why did she run out through the jib door?" George said.

"She's embarrassed about her weight," Bess put in. "I know how that feels. Abby just doesn't want to be caught eating something fattening like cake."

"Girls!" Rose's voice rang through the kitchen. "Is that you?"

"We're in the dining room," Nancy called.

Rose entered, followed by Hannah and Abby. Hannah and Rose were in their bathrobes, but Abby was still in her clothes.

"I heard a noise," Rose said. "I met Hannah and Abby in the hall. They heard it, too. Why is the jib door open?"

"We may have had an intruder," Nancy told Rose, "a hungry intruder. I'll show you." Nancy led the group back to the kitchen. She pointed to the cake plate now sitting on the kitchen table.

Hannah stared at the cake with the metal file lying across the plate. "Someone broke in to steal a piece of cake?" she said in disbelief.

"Why would someone cut the cake with a file?" Rose asked.

Nancy pointed at the empty space where the drawer of kitchen utensils usually was. "Maybe the file was the only utensil in sight," she suggested.

"That looks like Charlie's file," Abby said, frowning. "Why was it in the kitchen? I'm positive I returned it to his tool kit."

Nancy nodded at Bess, who handed the purple scarf to Abby. "My scarf!" Abby exclaimed. Then she blushed sheepishly. "Oh, now I remember. I felt better so I decided to varnish the table tonight, and I opened the jib door to get fresh air. I went out to the yard for a minute. I bet that's when I dropped my scarf. I guess I forgot to close the door when we all went to the saloon. I'm so sorry."

From the corner of her eye, Nancy could see Bess and George look at her. Abby's reaction seemed genuine. Maybe this was simply a case of an intruder coming through the open jib door. But why would an intruder steal only a piece of cake?

"It's all right," Rose told Abby wearily. "But please be more careful next time." She turned to Nancy. "Was anything else taken?"

"I don't think so," Nancy said. "The thief probably ran when the chair tipped over, afraid that the noise would wake us up."

Rose sighed. "Thank goodness. Why don't we all just get to bed?"

"Good idea," Nancy said. She and George closed the jib door, and the whole group headed back upstairs. On the way up, Nancy turned to Rose. "By the way, Rose, I forgot to tell you," she said. "George went running with Mary Lee this afternoon, and she said she'd give us a tour of Chinatown tomorrow. If we start working early in the morning, can we take off at two?"

"Of course, Nancy," Rose said.

"I have to get up early, too," Abby said. "I have to take my car in for a tune-up."

Good, Nancy thought. This would be their chance to search Abby's room.

The next morning the girls were pulling on their old jeans when they heard the front door slam. Nancy looked out the window to see Abby get into her little green car. "Let's go," she said.

Outside Abby's room, Nancy asked Bess to keep watch. "Abby shouldn't come back, but if she does, sneeze," she directed Bess. "Sneeze loudly so we can hear."

"Will do," Bess agreed.

Nancy and George stole into the room, shutting the door behind them. They began to search the room systematically. "No sign of Lizzie's papers," Nancy said after a while. "But I found this on her nightstand." She held out a magazine called *Magic.*

"I saw something like that, too." George went to Abby's bureau, retrieving a flyer advertising Silken Wonders Magic Studio.

"So Abby's into magic," Nancy mused.

"Doesn't surprise me," George commented. "She's always yakking about spirits and auras."

Nancy bent down to look under Abby's dressing table. She spied a small metal cylinder with a label that said Compressed Air. Behind the cylinder lay something that looked like a belt. Picking it up, she realized it was some kind of shoulder harness made of black fabric straps. She looked back and forth from the cylinder to the harness. What could Abby be using this equipment for?

Nancy stood up. George was sniffing Abby's perfumes on the dressing table. She smiled and handed one bottle to Nancy.

Nancy inhaled the fragrance. "Good work, George," she said. "Gardenia—the same fragrance as was on the note left on our pillowcase."

Just then Bess sneezed loudly.

"Abby's back!" George whispered.

"Quick, hide in the closet," Nancy said. She and George raced across the room until Bess popped her head in. "Sorry, false alarm," she confessed. "I couldn't help it. I really had to sneeze!"

Nancy giggled. "That's okay—we're done anyway," she said. "Let's go eat breakfast."

Mary was waiting for the girls at the bus stop near Portsmouth Square. "Hi! Welcome to Chinatown," she called out when she spotted them.

"Thanks for showing us around, Mary," Nancy said as she hopped off the bus.

"Don't mention it," Mary said. "After we walk around, my grandfather wants you to come to our restaurant for a meal. He has some pictures of my great-grandfather he thought you'd like to see."

"We'd love to," Bess said enthusiastically.

Mary and the girls walked through Portsmouth Square with its clusters of men playing chess and cards. "If you come in the morning, early, you'll see people performing t'ai chi here," Mary said.

"What's that clicking sound?" Nancy asked.

"The sound of mah-jongg tiles," Mary replied. "Mah-jongg's a very popular Chinese game. You can hear that sound all over Chinatown."

Their first stop was a ginseng store, where women sat behind the counter sorting odd-shaped roots. The girls tried cups of ginseng tea.

"Oooh!" Bess made a face as she sipped.

"It's good for you, Bess," Nancy teased.

Mary nodded. "Ginseng is supposed to help you live longer and be healthier," she explained.

Bess sighed. "Of course. If it tastes bad, it has to be good for you," she complained. Mary laughed.

The girls followed Mary through the crowded streets and alleyways of Chinatown. Roasted ducks hung in the windows of the many food stores, and fruit and vegetables lay in crates outside. Everyone around them was speaking rapidly in Chinese.

As they walked down Grant Avenue, George craned her neck up. "All these buildings look like pagodas!" she remarked. "See their curved roofs? And they're all painted red and green."

"After the 1906 earthquake," Mary explained, "the buildings here were all rebuilt in this style. It made new immigrants feel at home."

"And the lampposts look like Chinese lanterns," Bess added. "Totally cool."

Next Mary took them to a fortune cookie factory. There they watched in fascination as a machine poured cookie batter into tiny circular pools on a revolving griddle. The workers picked up each soft cookie from the turning griddle, placed a fortune inside, and sealed the cookie, bending it into the familiar curved shape.

When the girls returned to the street, they were all munching fortune cookies. Nancy read her fortune aloud. " 'Dark clouds will part and the answers will come.' "

" 'The rainbow follows the rain,' " read Bess.

George read hers: " 'Trust yourself, not a fortune cookie.' " The girls laughed.

"My turn," said Mary. " 'Many new friends will enter your life.' " She smiled. "They already have." She checked her watch. "Let's head over to see my grandfather."

Back on Grant Avenue, Mary led them up a stairway to the restaurant. A sign over the door read Phoenix Garden Restaurant.

The phoenix symbol was certainly showing up a lot in this case, Nancy thought to herself. The mantel at the Lees' other restaurant, the tower ornament on the mansion, the mirror in the saloon, and the song from *The Bandit's Treasure* mentioned a phoenix, too.

Inside the restaurant, Mary's uncle and grandfather greeted them warmly. They all sat down at a window table and enjoyed some delicious chicken and broccoli with garlic sauce.

When everyone had finished, Mary's grandfather rose and left the table, returning with a lacquer box. "My father," he said, "like many Chinese, came to California to find gold." He took a stack of photos and papers from the box. "California was called Gum San—Land of the Golden Mountain. But like many others, my father did not find riches in the gold country, only prejudice against the Chinese miners.

"So he came to San Francisco and worked at Lizzie's hotel," Mr. Lee went on. "He sent the money he earned home to his family."

"Your mother stayed in China?" Nancy asked.

Mr. Lee nodded. "My mother could not join him because of the immigration laws," he explained. "My parents were separated for twenty years."

Bess gasped. "How awful!"

Mr. Lee showed them a photograph of his father panning for gold and another of his father and mother. "And this is one of my favorites," he said, passing the photograph to Nancy. It showed Mary's great-grandfather standing with Lizzie Applegate in front of an ornate carved mantel.

"Was this taken at the hotel?" Nancy asked.

"Yes," Mr. Lee said.

"But this looks like the mantel in your other restaurant on California Street," Nancy said.

"That mantel was originally at the hotel," Mr. Lee explained. "Lizzie gave it to my father when she died."

"I'd love to have a copy of this picture," Bess said. "I'm making a display for the hotel. This picture would be the perfect centerpiece."

Mr. Lee promised Bess he would have a copy of the old photograph made for her right away.

Nancy, George, and Bess thanked Mary and her grandparents for their wonderful day in Chinatown. As the girls stood up to leave, Mary's grandfather spoke to her in Chinese. Mary looked surprised.

"What is it?" Nancy asked.

"My grandfather remembered something else about Lizzie's hotel," Mary said. "Once, late at night, when he was a little boy, he heard his father talking with his mother. His father called the hotel Gum Bo Fu."

"What does that mean?" Bess asked.

Mary's eyes sparkled. "Gum Bo Fu," she translated, "means 'Gold Treasure Mansion'!"

11

Disguise and Pursuit

"Gold Treasure Mansion!" Bess exclaimed as the girls returned to Grant Avenue. "You know what that means?"

George nodded. "It means that all that gold El Diablo was supposed to have stolen might have ended up with Lizzie at her hotel!"

"It's an interesting clue," Nancy admitted. "But it's just a name that a little boy overheard many, many years ago. We have no proof that it means what we'd like it to mean."

Bess sighed. "I suppose you're right, Nan."

"Here's the bus stop," Nancy said, checking her watch. "Time to head home."

Bess looked pained. "So soon?" she complained. "I was hoping to do a little shopping. All we've done on this trip is work."

"Shopping for what?" George asked.

"We need hats to wear with our dresses at the Winter Festival," Bess said. "We never did get to those stores on Sacramento Street."

Nancy looked uneasy. "I don't want to be away from the house too long," she said. "Not with all of these accidents going on."

"Why don't you go, then, Nan," George said. "I'll go with Bess and try to keep her out of trouble." She poked her cousin playfully in the shoulder.

Nancy boarded the next bus that came by, while Bess and George waited for one that would take them closer to Sacramento Street.

When Nancy walked in the door of the mansion, she heard the piano down in the saloon playing a bouncy ragtime tune. That must be Abby, Nancy figured.

Nancy walked through the entry hall, heading for the stairs down to the saloon. Just then, through the glass door at the back of the entry, she saw Abby come up the saloon stairs and go into the kitchen.

But the piano playing continued.

If Abby was upstairs, Nancy wondered, then who was playing the piano?

Nancy headed on down to the saloon. Halfway down the stairs, she heard the music stop.

When Nancy entered the saloon, it was empty. "Hello!" she called. No answer. Puzzled, she went over to the piano.

It looked like a regular grand piano. She pressed the keys and played a scale. Then she lifted the lid. Inside was a roll of music.

That's it! Nancy thought, a player piano. She'd

seen those before, though usually they were upright pianos. But this grand piano had a roll of music tucked away in its belly.

Nancy felt foolish. With all the weird goings-on in this house, my suspicions are on overdrive, she told herself.

Just then she heard voices on the saloon stairs. She hastily ducked behind the piano.

"Just consider my offer, Rose. I'm willing to buy you and Abby out." Nancy recognized Louis's voice speaking.

"Abby has already talked to me about selling the mansion," Rose answered as they came into the saloon. "And I won't."

"But the accidents," Louis said. "I'm worried about the danger—and the expense."

"We're making progress," Rose said stubbornly.

Nancy could hear Louis sigh. "I hope you're not being too optimistic," he warned. "If you lose your life savings, you don't have thirty working years to earn the money back, as Abby does. I'm willing to buy you out as an act of friendship. Think about it."

Silence. "I'll talk to Abby," Rose said at last in a small, tight voice.

So Rose is finally considering selling the house, Nancy thought to herself. But she can't give up, not now! Nancy clenched her jaw, more determined than ever to find out who was behind all these accidents. It would be so unfair if somebody else found Lizzie's gold.

Rose bent over Charlie's tool kit and took out a pair of pliers. "Here they are," she said. She and Louis left the saloon. Nancy waited a few minutes, then slipped quietly up the stairs, so no one would know she'd been down there.

Upstairs, she found Bess and George in the kitchen. "We found some fabulous hats," Bess said. "I spotted them from the window of the bus."

"You've never seen someone ring for a bus stop as fast as Bess did when she saw those hats in the window," George told Nancy.

"We'll show them to you later," Bess told Nancy. "Right now it's our turn to fix dinner." She handed Nancy an apron.

"What's on the menu?" Nancy asked.

"I'm making a cheese soufflé," Bess said. "You and George can do salad and dessert."

The three of them got busy. Bess took charge, bossing Nancy and George around, enjoying every minute of her role as head cook.

The cheese soufflé was a great success, as was Nancy's spinach salad and George's apple strudel. After dinner, despite Hannah's and Rose's protests, the girls insisted on washing up.

"You've been waiting on us enough," Bess said. "It's our turn to wait on you."

After cleaning up, the girls headed up to the Blue Room. On the bed Bess had laid out the dresses they'd found in the trunk. Then, from a large plastic bag, she pulled out a big feathered hat.

"Do you like it, Nancy?" Bess asked, settling the hat delicately on top of her blond hair.

"It does look nice," Nancy said, hiding a smile as she watched Bess's eagerness. Even when they had been little girls playing together, Bess had always enjoyed dress-up games.

"I feel just like Lizzie Applegate," Bess declared, admiring herself in the mirror. "We found hats for you and George, too."

Wordlessly, George held them up for Nancy to see—a wide-brimmed hat with black plumes and a tiny blue bonnet topped with a wispy mass of colored straw. Nancy and George rolled their eyes at each other behind Bess's back.

"You have to try on your dresses tonight," Bess insisted. "Lizzie was a big woman. I may have to take her dresses in to fit you or shorten them." Bess glanced at George's and Nancy's slender frames.

George groaned. "I know what that means."

"That's right," Bess said. "Time for a fitting session. Now change into those dresses." She flounced off to the hall bathroom to pin up her hair.

Nancy and George slipped out of their clothes and pulled on the heavy, old-fashioned dresses. Nancy chose a deep purple dress, George, the black-and-crimson one.

"The black-plumed hat goes best with my dress," George said, snatching it up.

"Yeah, thanks." Nancy laughed. "Now I'm stuck with this one that looks like a bird's nest!"

"Ouch!" George cried out, jerking her hand away from her hat. "What's this?" She pulled out a large hat pin.

"You'll need that to anchor the hat to your head," Nancy explained. "But be careful—those things can be dangerous."

Suddenly the bedroom door flew open. "Nancy! George! Come quick!" Bess shouted.

"What is it?" Nancy asked, already in motion.

Bess was streaking toward the bathroom. "I was looking out the window to see the full moon," she called over her shoulder, "and guess what I saw in the backyard. A blond woman with a small white dog! I think it's the ghost of Lizzie with her little dog. Hurry!"

Nancy and George ran after Bess. From the small bathroom window, Nancy could just make out a blond figure down in the garden, under a tree. The person seemed to be staring up at the moon. A small white dog sat on the ground beside her.

"I don't believe that's Lizzie," Nancy said, "but I do want to know who it is. Let's go!"

Still in their antique dresses, the three girls rustled downstairs and raced out into the backyard. The yard was empty and still.

"Where did she go?" Bess asked.

The girls listened and looked. With the light of the full moon, they could see very clearly. No one was there. Then they heard footsteps.

Mary Lee came around the corner of the

house. "Oh!" She jumped in fright when she saw the girls. "What are *you* dressed for?"

"Winter Festival," Bess answered simply. "But Mary, what are you doing here?"

"Uh . . . I'm—I'm looking for my cat," Mary said, flustered. "Max, my Manx cat. Have you seen him?"

A loud rustling came from the base of the house, and a cat ran out of the shrubbery. "Max!" Mary called. "See you guys later!" she added hastily, and then ran off after the cat.

George looked at Nancy. "A Manx cat doesn't have a tail," George said slowly. "But I definitely saw a tail on that cat. It looked like Abby's black cat, Alfreida."

"Where did the cat come from?" Nancy wondered. Gathering up her long skirts, she poked around the overgrown bushes at the base of the mansion.

"Hey, look." She held up a screen from one of the saloon's ventilation windows. "The cat was probably trapped inside. When he ran out, the screen fell off. That's the noise we heard."

Nancy propped the screen against the house and the girls headed back inside. "Well, at least you saw Lizzie from the window," Bess said.

"Well, we saw *someone,*" Nancy admitted.

Back in the Blue Room, the dress fitting began. Bess sat on the armchair in their bedroom's side nook, taking in the side seams of George's dress. "Please hold still, George," Bess pleaded.

"You're sticking me!" George said.

"If you'd stop wiggling, I wouldn't have to," Bess mumbled through a mouthful of pins. "Now bend over so I can get this back waist seam."

"I can't stand this much longer," George muttered. Bending forward from the waist, she leaned her hands for support against the paneled wall beside her.

"Lean over a little more," Bess directed her.

George bent further, pushing against the wall.

The oak panels creaked and trembled. Then, with a groan, a secret door slowly swung open.

12

The Spirits Speak

George stumbled forward as the paneling gave way. "Whoa!" she yelled. "What—"

Nancy ran over, while Bess spit out the pins from her mouth. "You must have pressed a secret lever, George," Nancy said.

George straightened up. "I was leaning right here," she said, pressing against one side of the wood panel. The door opened wider. "Look!"

Behind the panel, in a dark niche, was a large, black, painted safe. George reached in and tugged on the safe's metal handles. "It's locked," she said.

"Give it a try, Nancy," Bess urged. "Lizzie's secret may be inside!"

Nancy fiddled with the combination lock for a few minutes, one ear pressed against the dial to listen to the tumblers. At last she heard a click, and the steel doors grated open.

Inside the safe was a brown accordion file tied

with black satin ribbon. Nancy pulled it out. "Let's look at it on the bed," she said.

"Hurry!" Bess said. "I can't wait."

Sitting cross-legged on the bed, Nancy untied the ribbon and opened the file. It was full of old papers. Nancy examined the first document, a small sheet with Certificate of Marriage printed in elegant lettering at the top. She handed it to Bess. "You'll like this, Bess."

Bess's eyes glowed as she read the certificate. "Diego and Lizzie were married on June 18, 1877, in Gold Pine Valley, California!"

"What else is there?" George asked Nancy.

Nancy's heart pounded as she flipped through the papers. "Mining stocks," she said, handing George several certificates with fancy embossed borders.

Bess picked up an old notebook and opened it. "Oh, it's Lizzie's journal!" She scanned the notebook pages. "And listen—this section is called 'Life as a Bandit'! So Lizzie Applegate really did join El Diablo's gang. Now we have proof."

"What about the gold?" George asked.

Bess flipped through blank pages. "The last entry is Christmas Eve, 1878."

"The day *before* the big stagecoach robbery," George observed.

Nancy picked up a handwritten document. She reached out to clutch Bess's arm. "This looks like a will! Signed by Elizabeth Valdez, and dated 1902."

"Read it, Nancy," George urged.

Nancy cleared her throat and read aloud. " 'I, Elizabeth Valdez, do hereby make this my last will and testament. To my employee and friend Lee Wing Yuen, the Chinese overmantel and the sum of fifteen thousand dollars.' "

"Mary's great-grandfather!" George said.

Nancy nodded and read on. " 'To Nellie Beecham, my emerald brooch and the sum of five thousand dollars.' "

"Maybe like the emerald brooch Louis has in his shop," Bess noted. "He said they were common."

Nancy scanned the rest of the will. "There are more bequests for smaller items," she said. "But listen to this: 'To my beloved husband, Diego Valdez, my house and its contents with the exception of the bequests above.' "

"I knew it!" Bess cried. "Diego was alive!"

Nancy held up her hand. "Maybe not," she said. "The will goes on to say that if Diego is deceased, the house is to be sold and the proceeds donated to charity. My guess is that Lizzie didn't know whether he was still alive."

"But I don't understand," George said. "If we're just finding this will now, how did Mary's grandfather get the Chinese mantel?"

"Maybe she also left it to him in another version of the will," Nancy noted. "This may not have been her final will. This is dated 1902, but she lived until 1906."

"Nancy, George, look at this—a telegram."
Bess said, holding up a small yellowed piece of
paper. " 'Dearest Gardenia: I will return.' The
telegram must be from Diego. How romantic!"

Nancy pointed to the top of the telegram. "It's
dated January 2, 1879—*after* the Christmas Day
robbery. So Diego did survive the ambush."

"But if Diego had come back," Bess reasoned,
"Lizzie wouldn't have been trying to reach him
through séances for years."

"Remember, some people thought Lizzie's
séances were publicity stunts," Nancy said.
"Maybe Diego did come back for the gold."

George was busy examining the other papers.
"These are house plans," she said. "And it sure
looks like the layout of this mansion."

Nancy eagerly took the faded drawings and
studied them. "The house has changed," she
said, tracing the drawings with her fingernail.
"Rose's office must have been added later. And
look—there was originally a fireplace in the
entry hall, here." She pointed.

"That's the wall where I'm going to put my
photo display," Bess said. "Ooh, wait until Rose
and Abby learn what we found tonight!"

George frowned. "Do you think Rose—or
Abby—already knows this safe is here?"

Nancy shook her head as she gathered up the
papers. "Even if they *had* found this secret door,
they probably couldn't have opened the lock.
Besides, Rose said to me they had no plans of the

109

house, so they must not have seen these. Let's keep these papers a secret for now," she cautioned her friends, "until we find the gold."

"Then you really do believe the gold is hidden here, in the mansion?" Bess asked.

Nancy hesitated. "Maybe it is, maybe it isn't," she hedged. "But I believe that *somebody* thinks it's here, and that person has been causing all these so-called accidents to scare Rose away."

Bess was looking through the journal one last time. Suddenly she gasped. "Listen to this—it's on the last page. She writes: 'Forever, Diego, your treasure I hold true'—just like the words in the song. The gold *must* be here!"

The next day at lunch, Nancy and Rose had just begun eating their tuna sandwiches when Abby walked into the kitchen. Nancy blinked, astonished. Abby wore a silver turban, a matching silver skirt, and a black satin jacket with flowing sleeves. Nancy could smell Abby's perfume— gardenia.

"Why, Abby," said Rose. "What on earth are you dressed up for?"

"I'd like to invite you to a séance," Abby said dramatically, "after lunch, in the saloon."

"Oh, no, Abby!" Rose protested. "We've got too much work to do. We don't have time for games."

Abby's face flushed. "It's not a game, Rose," she insisted. "To make this bed-and-breakfast a

110

success, we have to stand out from the crowd. Séances could attract a lot of people."

Rose hesitated. "Well, all right," she said, giving in. "But then we all have to get back to work."

After lunch the girls, Hannah, and Rose followed Abby to the dark saloon. At the top of the stairs Abby paused to take a candle from her jacket pocket and light it. Then she led them in a candlelit procession down the stairs.

Chairs were set around a square wooden table by the piano. Several books lay on one corner of the table. "Please sit down," Abby said, putting the candle in the candlestick on the piano.

Once everyone had sat down, Abby was silent for a few minutes. Nancy felt restless. A séance seemed like a waste of time, except that she might learn something about Abby from it.

"We will attempt to contact the spirits," Abby said at last, her voice low and solemn. "Join hands on the table." Abby began to hum softly. "Is there a spirit you wish to contact?"

"Lizzie Applegate," Bess announced.

"Lizzie Applegate," Abby repeated. "Lizzie Applegate. We ask for a sign. Spirits, speak!"

Suddenly, a rapping noise broke the silence. It seemed to come from the table.

"The spirits are here," Abby said. "Lizzie, is that you? One rap for no, three for yes."

There was a momentary silence, followed by three distinct raps.

"Lizzie's here!" Bess squealed. "Is Diego here, too?"

One rap. No.

Suddenly a dog began barking. "That's Lizzie's dog," Bess said. But just then Bess's chair lurched forward. She screamed, grabbing the chair with both hands to keep herself upright.

Now the table began to rock back and forth, first gently and then with more force. The books fell with a resounding thump. Then one end of the table rose and stayed up in the air.

"Oh!" Bess gasped.

The table fell with a thud. Abruptly, the piano burst out with a jangling tune.

Nancy felt Hannah grip her hand tightly. She glanced at Hannah, who rolled her eyes, looking annoyed by Abby's theatrics.

Abby rose and began to circle the room. Moving over by the bar, she was barely visible. Nancy heard a whooshing sound like wind coming through a tunnel. A silver-colored spirit seemed to float through the air above Abby.

Nancy stifled a grin. That was the same figure she had seen floating in the fog outside Abby's window her first night here. So that's what the equipment in Abby's room was for!

Gradually, the spirit vanished. Abby circled the room, calling, "Speak to us, Lizzie."

Returning to the table, Abby took the candle and a piece of paper from the piano. "We will ask for another message," she said. She held the paper above the candle flame. The paper burned with a startling white flash.

"The spirits have finished!" Abby proclaimed. "The séance is over!" Holding the candlestick, Abby began walking to the top of the stairs.

"Is that it?" George said flatly.

Nancy shrugged. "I guess so." She and George followed Hannah, Bess, and Rose upstairs.

Abby seemed to have vanished when they got upstairs. Hannah, Rose, and the girls trooped into the parlor. "Well, that was something," George said, dropping onto the larger sofa.

"Lizzie was really here!" Bess exclaimed. She turned to Nancy. "Now do you believe in Lizzie's ghost?"

"That was a magic show, Bess," Rose said. "Abby has always loved magic and illusions."

Bess gave a huge sigh of frustration.

"With the right equipment, we could reproduce every one of those effects," Nancy added. "The floating spirit was just a balloon, the same balloon I saw the other night outside Abby's window. I guarantee you that under her loose clothing, Abby has a cylinder of compressed air with a tube attached, leading to the balloon." She and George exchanged glances, recalling the cylinder they'd found in Abby's room.

"What about the piano?" Hannah asked.

"The piano is a player piano," Nancy explained, "hooked up to a timer maybe. And the magic paper that burned in a flash could be bought at any magic store."

113

"But the rapping table?" Bess asked.

"Mediums have been producing rapping tables for years," Nancy told her. "You could simply have a block of wood strapped to your leg, which you bang against a table leg. I don't know exactly how Abby made the table jerk and your chair lurch. Maybe she's got some kind of mechanical device."

Bess crossed her arms. "Well, I still think Lizzie really was here," she said stubbornly.

Just then the doorbell rang. Nancy went to open the door. Mary Lee was there. "Hi, Nancy," she said. "I brought you that copy of the photo of my great-grandfather with Lizzie."

Bess came up behind Nancy. "Hi, Mary. Did you ever find your cat?"

Mary looked embarrassed. "Oh, uh, yes."

"Good," Bess said brightly. "Want to come up and get a better look at our dresses?" As she led Mary upstairs, Bess flashed Nancy a look to say she'd pump Mary about the night before in the garden.

"Well, back to work," George groaned, joining Nancy in the entry. "I've still got half the yard to rake."

"I'll join you in a minute," Nancy said.

Checking that Hannah and Rose were still in the parlor, Nancy quietly slipped downstairs to the saloon. Flipping on the light, she went over to examine the séance table.

Nancy bent down to study the legs of the table. Underneath the third leg, she saw, the floor-

114

boards were raised just slightly. Had they been knocked loose?

Then, looking closer, she noticed with a frown that they all ended in a straight line instead of ending unevenly at different lengths.

Nancy's mouth dropped open. Those weren't loose floorboards she was looking at.

It was a trapdoor!

13

The Secret Tunnel

Her heart racing, Nancy pushed aside the table and lifted the trapdoor. Underneath was a small, dark tunnel. Was this Abby's secret?

Her skin tingling with excitement, Nancy jumped up to get a flashlight. She spied Charlie's tool kit in the corner of the saloon and quickly found a flashlight in it.

She turned on the flashlight and climbed down through the trapdoor. A dirt-floored tunnel stretched before her. Curious, Nancy crawled forward.

About fifteen feet farther on, the tunnel turned sharply. Nancy flashed her light up and found a narrow square hole above her head. Crawling up through it, she found herself in a small room. Nancy turned around and found herself staring into the lighted saloon.

She gasped. The wall of this little room must be the back side of the mirror over the saloon's bar. Another trick mirror, like the one between the parlor and entry hall upstairs! Switching off the flashlight, she could see into the saloon even more clearly.

Why would Lizzie have built this hiding space with the trick mirror? Then it dawned on Nancy. This would be the perfect place for Lizzie to spy on the activities in her saloon.

Then Nancy remembered the night Bess had "seen" Lizzie in the mirror. If this mirror was a two-way mirror, someone must have been standing in this little room.

But who was it?

Suddenly, Nancy heard a quiet whimpering. She spun around, turning on the flashlight.

In a corner of the closetlike chamber, a white puppy gazed at her with huge sad eyes. A blood-stained rag was wrapped around his right paw. Beside him was a dish of water, a sleeping bag, and an empty Chinese food take-out carton.

It looked as if someone was living in this little room with this puppy, but who?

The puppy whimpered and then barked. "It's okay," Nancy said to him softly. "Don't be afraid." She knelt down and examined the dog's badly cut paw.

Then she swept her flashlight around the little room. In one corner a ladder led to a door overhead. She climbed up and pushed on the door. It wouldn't budge.

Nancy tried to visualize the layout of the house. If this hiding space was behind the saloon mirror, then it must also be beneath the pantry, right where the girls had moved the heavy ceramic crocks! That's what was blocking this door, probably. Before the crocks were moved, someone might have been using this ladder to get into the kitchen and steal food.

Just then a sharp scratching noise came from a side wall. Nancy shone the flashlight over. She saw a ventilation window with a sturdy cardboard box placed underneath so someone could climb in and out. Nancy realized what the scraping noise was: George raking leaves in the back garden.

"George!" Nancy called.

The rake stopped. "Nancy?"

"Look for the window," Nancy yelled.

Nancy could hear the heavy shrubbery rustling. Then George peered through the small window. "Where *are* you, Nancy?" she asked, sounding baffled.

"I'll explain later," Nancy said. "But first, take the puppy." She lifted him up through the window.

"Puppy?" George said, surprised. She took him gently in her arms.

"I'll meet you out front," Nancy said.

She crawled back out through the tunnel and ran upstairs to the Blue Room. Mary and Bess were sitting on the bed, admiring the old-fashioned dresses and hats.

"Mary, you have a cat," Nancy said as she burst into the room. "Is there a veterinarian anywhere nearby?"

"Why, yes," Mary said. "Dr. McGuire. She's on Pine Street, one block away. But what—"

"I'll tell you later," Nancy said, grabbing her jacket and purse and running back downstairs to find George and the puppy.

While walking to the vet's, Nancy told George what she had found. "That hiding space behind the mirror explains a few things," she said. "That's why the food was disappearing from the kitchen. And Bess's vision of Lizzie in the mirror was probably that person standing in the chamber."

"So maybe that's who is creating all the accidents," George said. "The falling window, the flood, the fire, the chandelier—"

Nancy looked doubtful. "Maybe," she said. "But we don't have any evidence yet."

Dr. McGuire, a young vet wearing blue jeans under her white coat, stitched up the dog's cut paw, put a bandage on it, and prescribed an ointment. "He'll be all right," the vet assured them. "But I'd like to see him in a week."

The girls walked back to the mansion, Nancy carrying the little dog. But as they turned onto California Street, footsteps pounded behind them and a voice shouted, "Hey! That's *my* dog!"

Nancy wheeled around to face the teenage boy in the ragged army jacket. His long blond hair fell in curls around his face.

Nancy and George looked at each other. So that's who was living in the secret room! With his long blond hair, no wonder Bess thought he was a woman dressed in men's clothes. And it was probably him out in the garden last night, too. So much for Bess's ghost.

The boy stood on the sidewalk, looking belligerent. Nancy gave him a friendly smile and held out the puppy. "We saw his paw was hurt, so we took him to the vet," she said kindly.

The boy took the dog awkwardly. "Uh, thanks," he said. "He stepped on a nail, and it cut him pretty bad. I wanted to take him to the doctor, but I don't have any money." He rubbed the dog behind the ears, and the puppy wagged his tail wildly. "I found him one day last week. Somebody threw him out, I guess. I call him Tramp, 'cause he's just a tramp, like me."

The boy's voice was steady, but his eyes shifted around nervously. Was he in trouble? Nancy wondered. "Who are you?" she asked. "And why are you hiding out in the mansion?"

The boy bit his lip. "My name's Tim Coletti," he said. "I just finished high school in Iowa this year and I came out to San Francisco. I've always wanted to live in a big city. But I didn't have a place to stay and . . . well, I guess I didn't plan on everything being so expensive. I ran out of money," he admitted. "I thought I could just crash in the old house. I didn't mean any harm."

"But that's trespassing," Nancy said.

Tim kept his eyes to the ground. "I know," he said. "But the place is so big, and I thought no one would notice. I'm sure neither of the ladies who own it know about the secret room."

"How did *you* find it?" George asked.

"A couple of weeks ago, I applied for a job washing dishes at the Chinese restaurant," Tim said. "It was raining that day and really cold, so I ducked under some bushes. The frame had fallen off that little window, so I crawled inside. I found that weird room, and I stayed."

"You work at the restaurant?" Nancy asked.

"On weekends," Tim said. "I'm saving money to get a place to live."

"Then you do know Mary?" George asked.

"Yeah," Tim said, smiling for the first time. "She's really nice. She gives me food, even on days I'm not working."

Now Nancy knew why Mary was in the garden the night before—she'd been bringing food to Tim. "You took food from our kitchen, too, right?" Nancy asked.

Tim squirmed. "Yeah—at least, until a few days ago, when the door got blocked," he said. "And the other night, when someone left the big window door open—"

"The jib door," George put in.

The boy shrugged. "I guess. I took some cake that night," he confessed. "It was really good."

"Why did you cut it with a file?" Nancy asked.

"I couldn't find a knife," Tim said. "But the file was lying on top of the refrigerator."

"One more thing," Nancy said to Tim. "The

121

day of the fire, I saw you running away from the mansion. Why?"

"I smelled smoke," he said simply. "I ran to pull the fire alarm on the corner."

"Did you have anything to do with starting the fire?" Nancy asked quietly.

Tim's blue eyes grew big. "No! I swear I didn't!" he insisted.

Nancy stared at him. He seemed to be telling the truth. "Did you see anything unusual before the fire started?" she asked.

Tim thought for a moment. "No—only . . . well, right before I smelled the smoke, I looked out my little window and saw that old guy."

"Charlie?" Nancy asked.

Tim looked blank. "Is that his name? The guy who's always around the house?" he said. "Anyway, he was carrying a red bag, like an old sports duffel. He was holding on real tight, like he was afraid to lose it."

Nancy's eyes widened in surprise. The sales slip from the building supply store seemed like a good alibi for Charlie. But had he really been at the mansion at the time of the fire?

Shifting from foot to foot, Tim looked at Nancy and George anxiously. "Look, are you guys going to make me leave the house? I don't have a place yet. Do you think—could Tramp and I stay a little longer?" he pleaded.

Nancy looked at George. She could tell her friend felt just as sorry for Tim as she did. "It might help to have another pair of eyes around,"

Nancy admitted. "We'll keep your secret—if you promise to tell us about anything unusual you see."

Tim broke out into a grateful grin. "Thanks!" he said. "And could you unblock that door? I won't take any food, but I'd like to be able to get water for me and Tramp."

Nancy nodded. "And we'll leave food out."

On returning to the house, Nancy and George went first to the pantry. They dragged the large ceramic crocks away from the trapdoor.

Then they went up to the Blue Room, where Bess had talked Mary into helping her alter the dresses. Nancy and George filled them in on what they'd learned. Mary said she was relieved not to have to keep Tim's secret anymore.

Mary had planned to go running with George, but one panicky look from Bess convinced her to stay and finish sewing. Nancy offered to go with George instead. They changed into jogging clothes.

As Nancy and George came out the front door, Louis was stepping out of his car, carrying a bouquet of yellow roses. "Roses for my Rose," he said. He winked at the girls and then waved as they started to jog off toward the Presidio.

Nancy and George ran in silence for several miles through the misty twilight. Fog gathered, and it grew dark rapidly. "Let's head home," Nancy suggested. George nodded, and they turned around.

Suddenly headlights cut through the mist. A

123

car swung around the bend ahead, going very fast. Nancy looked up, expecting the car to swerve around them.

But as the headlights came closer, Nancy gasped. The car wasn't swerving at all. It was heading straight for them!

14

Too Close!

"Watch it!" Nancy yelled. She pushed George into the large bushes bordering the sidewalk and jumped in after her.

The headlights glared into the bushes, and the piercing squeal of tires cut through the night air. Peering through the bushes, Nancy saw the car barely miss the sidewalk as it screeched around the bend and roared off into the gathering dusk.

Nancy's eyes widened in fear and disbelief. The car was a Bay City Cab, number 78.

George rose, brushing off dirt and leaves. "That was close!"

"Too close," Nancy said, standing up.

"I guess that driver didn't see us because of the fog," George said.

"I think the driver of that car *did* see us," Nancy said firmly. "It headed right for us. But it veered off at the last minute, as if he only wanted to scare us." She drew a breath. "It was a Bay

City Cab, George. Charlie drives a Bay City Cab."

George stared at Nancy. "Was it him?"

"I don't know," Nancy said. "But I know how to find out."

The girls jogged back to the mansion. Nancy bolted up the stairs, ran to the Blue Room, and got Lieutenant Chin's card from her purse. Then she went back down to the kitchen phone to dial his number.

"You said to call if I needed help, Lieutenant," she said as he picked up the line.

"What can I do for you, Nancy?" he asked.

"I need to know who was driving Bay City Cab number seventy-eight this evening," Nancy said.

"I'm sure I can get that information," he said, sounding puzzled. "But why? Is this a police matter?"

"It may be, Lieutenant. The cab tried to run us down just now," Nancy told him.

Lieutenant Chin paused. "You're sure the driver just didn't see you?" he said cautiously.

"It's possible, but I don't think so," Nancy replied.

"I'll get you the information," the police detective assured her. "I trust your instincts. But, Nancy, please be careful. And when it's time, you must call in the authorities."

"I know that, Lieutenant," Nancy said.

"Good. I'll get back to you," he said.

* * *

126

The next morning, when the girls came down to breakfast, Louis was sitting at the kitchen table with Rose and Abby. Louis looked handsome in a nubbly gray sports jacket and charcoal gray slacks.

"Good morning," Nancy said, grabbing a container of yogurt from the refrigerator. "Where's Hannah?"

"She's having Sunday brunch with her friend Emily," Rose said. "They're going to try out the omelettes at the café in the Miramar Hotel."

Abby smiled. "Those omelettes are heavenly."

"So are you girls interested in helping me set up my booth for the Winter Festival?" Louis asked. "The festival starts at noon, so we have to decorate this morning."

"I'd really better keep working with Charlie on chipping the paint outside," Nancy said, begging off. It would be a perfect chance to ask Charlie some questions, she thought.

"Count me out," Abby said. "I'm going to start sanding the saloon floor. Charlie rented a sander. It'll be a big job, so if I can get in even a few hours of work this morning, that will be one step forward."

"Well, I'm happy to help with the booth," George said. "So is Bess. Right, Bess?"

"Sounds better than wallpapering," Bess chimed in, flashing a mischievous smile as she poured herself a bowl of granola.

"Good," Louis said. "I'll drop you off here

after we're done so you can change into your costumes." He paused. "Won't you reconsider, Nancy? It should be loads of fun. I have a collection of antique ornaments in the car, a little tree, and a whole assortment of curio items. We'll make the booth look just like a little Victorian shop, all decorated for Christmas."

Nancy shook her head. "Thanks, but no thanks. I'll see you all back here."

Rose placed her hand on Louis's. "I'm glad to help," she murmured. "I know I'll enjoy it."

Louis gave her fingers a gentle tug. "It'll do you good to get out of the mansion for a while," he told her in a soft, husky voice.

The telephone rang, and Nancy hopped up to get it. At the other end was Lieutenant Chin. "Nancy? I have the name of the driver of cab seventy-eight last night," he told her. "It was a Charles Webber."

Nancy's heart jumped. It *was* Charlie! "Uh, I see. Thank you," she quickly said, turning her face away so no one in the kitchen could see her flush.

"If there's anything else I can do, Nancy, please let me know," Lieutenant Chin said. "And remember—don't take any chances."

"I won't," Nancy promised.

As Nancy hung up, Louis rubbed his hands together and said briskly, "Everybody ready?"

Rose laughed. "Louis! I'm still drinking my coffee!"

Within ten minutes, however, Louis, Rose,

Bess, and George had piled into Louis's silver sedan and left. Abby disappeared into the saloon. Nancy grabbed her coat, went outside, climbed up on the scaffolding, and began stripping paint again.

An hour later Abby stuck her head out a nearby window. "Is Charlie there?" she asked.

"No, Abby," Nancy said, halting her work.

"I wonder where he is," Abby fretted. "He should be here with the sander by now. He's absolutely never late."

Nancy thoughtfully tapped her paint scraper against a scaffolding pipe. If Charlie *was* the one who had started the fire and caused the other accidents, she reasoned, then he'd be getting very nervous by now. He might try something really dangerous!

Making a decision, Nancy collected her tools. "Let me go to Louis's store," she suggested. "Charlie's daughter, Cassandra, works there. Maybe she knows where he is."

Nancy trotted quickly over to Chandler Interiors. Little bells over the door tinkled when Nancy entered the shop, but no one appeared at the counter.

Nancy heard Cassandra's voice in the back. "All right. I'll do it!" she was saying. Then Nancy heard the phone slam down.

Cassandra ran out from the back room, her lower lip trembling. She gave a start when she saw Nancy and quickly brushed tears from her cheeks. Bowing her head low, she hurriedly began sorting through papers behind the counter.

Nancy went to the counter. "What is it, Cassandra? Are you all right?" she asked.

Cassandra, still sniffling, nodded.

Nancy reached out for the girl's hand. "Is there anything I can do?" Nancy asked gently.

Cassandra yanked back her hand and shook her head no.

Nancy wasn't sure what to do. The girl was obviously upset, but she didn't seem to want Nancy's help. "Look, I won't stay long," Nancy said. "I just wondered if you knew where your father is. We expected him at the mansion today."

Cassandra shook her head once more and blew her nose with a tissue. "I don't know," she muttered, not looking at Nancy. "I have to go now." She wheeled around and darted back to the rear office.

Nancy left the store wondering what Cassandra was so worked up about. Could it be something to do with her father?

Nancy returned to the mansion and walked into the entry hall, deep in thought. Standing beside one of the built-in carved benches, she looked down. There lay the photo Mary Lee had brought the day before—the one of her great-grandfather and Lizzie Applegate in front of the carved mantel.

Nancy stood still and stared at it hard. Something in her mind clicked. The house plans they'd found in the safe the other night showed a fireplace in the entry hall. That must have been where the carved mantel had been. She looked over and spotted the wall where the fireplace must have been located, right across from the front door.

Nancy walked over to the wall. She pulled back the canvas tarp covering the floor.

The floorboards just in front of the wall had a slightly different color and wood grain than the other floorboards, as if they hadn't been part of the original flooring. That made sense, Nancy thought. When the fireplace was removed, a new patch of floorboards must have been laid to fill in the gap.

Suddenly Abby came rushing out from the back hall. "Nancy! The desk clerk at the Miramar just called," she said breathlessly. "Hannah is ill! She wants you to pick her up."

Nancy looked at Abby in alarm. Hannah? Hannah was never sick! "Did the clerk say what was wrong?" she asked.

"No, just that Hannah had become ill very suddenly," Abby said. She looked genuinely concerned. "You take my car," Abby offered. "Or do you want me to go with you?"

"No, stay here," Nancy said. "With all the accidents, someone should watch the house."

"All right then," Abby said. "Here are the keys." She fished a key chain from her skirt pocket and tossed it to Nancy. "The car's in good shape. I got new brakes a few months back, and the engine just had a tune-up two days ago. But the Miramar is in the steepest part of town. Are you okay driving on steep hills?"

"I've driven the hills of San Francisco before," Nancy said. "Thanks, I'll be careful."

Following Abby's directions to the Miramar, Nancy drove Abby's little green car downtown, fighting back waves of anxiety. She found a parking space near the entrance and pulled in. She ran past the taxis and limousines waiting right in front of the hotel, past the doormen dressed in top hats, and into the red-carpeted lobby.

But just as she swung around a tall Christmas tree, she ran right into Hannah's arms. "Nancy! What on earth are you doing here?" Hannah asked.

Nancy hugged Hannah. "Oh, Hannah! You're all right," she gasped in relief. "I was so worried. What happened?"

"What are you talking about, dear?" Hannah asked. Emily Foxworth came up beside her. "We've just had the most lovely breakfast," Hannah said. "Cheese omelettes with wonderful fried potatoes. Emily was about to give me a ride home."

"I gave Hannah that article for you—the one I mentioned about gold treasure hunters," Emily added. Hannah reached into her purse and pulled out several photocopied pages.

Nancy frowned. "Thank you, Emily," she said

absently, taking the article and tucking it in her purse. "But, Hannah, the desk clerk called the mansion a little while ago saying that you'd gotten quite ill."

"What?" Hannah said indignantly. "I'm quite well, thank you!"

Nancy went to check at the front desk, then at the café, to see if anyone on the staff had made a telephone call about Hannah Gruen's illness. No one knew anything about it.

Her mouth set in a grim line, Nancy walked across the lobby to rejoin Hannah and Emily. Maybe this was just a ruse to get me away from the mansion, she thought. Had someone called, pretending to be the desk clerk? Or had Abby simply made up her story about receiving a phone call?

"I'll ride home with Nancy, then," Hannah was saying to Emily when Nancy returned.

On the way to the car, Nancy shared her concerns with Hannah. "Someone wanted me out of the mansion," she declared. "That must have been the reason for the phony phone call. There could be trouble waiting for us back at the house."

"We'll be careful," Hannah said.

They got into Abby's car, and Nancy pulled away from the curb into the heavy traffic. She guided the green car over the top of the hill and started down the steep incline. Stepping on the brakes, she shifted the car into low gear. She let up the brake, then pressed down again. But when she pressed on the pedal this time, nothing happened.

Nancy raised her foot and stepped on the brake again. Nothing!

"Nancy! Slow down!" Hannah cried, gripping the dashboard.

"I'm trying!" Nancy exclaimed.

Adrenaline shot through Nancy's body as she furiously pumped the brake pedal.

The car had no brakes!

15

The Clue in the Photograph

Nancy wrapped her fingers around the steering wheel. "Hannah, hang on!" she said, her voice breaking with fear.

The car was gaining speed. Nancy yanked on the emergency brake. The car wrenched and slowed momentarily, but the brake couldn't stop it.

Then Nancy saw her chance: an empty stretch of curb and a lamppost. "Hang on!" she yelled again.

Nancy threw the wheel sharply to the right. As the bumper hit the metal lamppost, the car came to a shuddering stop. The crash sent shock waves through Nancy's body.

Nancy released her fierce grip on the steering wheel. "Hannah, are you all right?" she asked.

Still clutching the dashboard, her face frozen in fear, Hannah didn't answer. Slowly she began to relax. "Yes, I'm fine, Nancy."

Nancy got out to examine the damage. The front corner of the car was badly dented, and green fluid poured from the engine.

Nancy's mind was racing. She suspected the car had been sabotaged. Abby had *said* she'd just had the car in for a tune-up. If there had been anything wrong, the mechanic would have noticed it then. That is, unless Abby had been lying.

On her hands and knees, Nancy looked under the car. She knew what she was looking for, and she found it.

The brake lines had been cut.

Nancy stood up slowly. Someone had tried to kill her and Hannah. Who?

Hannah was sitting back in her seat, resting. "I'm going to call a tow truck," Nancy said. "I'll run back and use the phone at the hotel. Will you be okay until I get back?" Hannah nodded. Nancy turned to start jogging back to the Miramar.

Just then a silver sedan came over the top of the steep hill. Louis!

Louis lightly tapped his horn, then pulled his car over to the curb. He jumped out and ran to join Nancy and Hannah.

"Louis!" Hannah exclaimed.

"Thank heaven you're both all right!" Louis said. "When I dropped off the girls at the mansion, Abby told me you'd fallen ill, Hannah. I rushed downtown to see if I could help. I'm glad your illness was a false alarm. But this!" Louis glanced at the crumpled fender of Abby's car. "What happened?"

Nancy hesitated. She wasn't sure how much to say to anyone now. "I lost control of the car somehow," she said. "These steep hills are so hard to drive on, you know. I was just about to call a tow truck."

"Here, I've got a car phone," Louis said. "I'll call the garage I always use. Let's have my mechanic take a look at the car."

Nancy was glad she'd said nothing about the brakes. This way, she'd get a full, unbiased report from Louis's mechanic. "All right," Nancy said.

After the tow truck arrived, Louis drove Nancy and Hannah back to the mansion. Shutting her eyes, Hannah sank into the plush red upholstery of the front seat. Nancy stared out the window in back.

But as Louis drove past the Miramar, Nancy glanced over at the line of taxis waiting for passengers in front of the hotel. There was Charlie, sitting in his green-and-white Bay City cab.

Charlie at the scene of an accident again! Nancy thought warily. Had he been the one who cut the brakes? And was all this connected to the other accidents?

As they drove up to the mansion, Nancy spotted Tim lounging on a neighbor's lawn. She made quick eye contact with him, and he gave her the slightest possible nod. Nancy was glad he was keeping an eye on things just as he'd promised.

"I'll feel better after my mechanic looks at Abby's car," Louis was saying in the front seat. "Yet another accident. And what if they *aren't* all accidents? After all, with sixty thousand dollars in 1878 gold coins at stake, who knows what could happen?" Distracted, Nancy hardly heard him.

At the mansion, Abby, George, and Bess were waiting anxiously. George and Bess were dressed in their Victorian gowns, while Abby wore a paisley skirt and white pirate's shirt with billowing sleeves. Hannah described the accident to them.

"You could have been killed!" Abby said. "Oh, I feel like it's my fault. But I just had the car checked thoroughly, and the mechanic said it was fine." She frowned and looked worried.

"Well, I'm just glad Hannah isn't sick and that you're both all right," Bess said, turning with a rustle of her long skirts. "But now, Nancy, you need to get dressed."

Nancy took a quick shower and then put on the greenish blue dress. As Bess helped Nancy fasten the many buttons of the dress, Nancy swiveled in front of the mirror. She had to admire Bess's alterations—the gown was a perfect fit.

The girls tucked themselves into the backseat of Louis's sedan, while Hannah and Abby sat up front. Bess and George chatted with Hannah, telling her about the booth they'd been decorating all morning.

Nancy, reaching in her purse for a comb, felt a

wad of folded paper and pulled it out. It was the article Emily had given her on treasure hunters. Her eyes skimmed over it. Then a name leapt out from the print: ". . . said Louis Chandler, gold treasure hunter . . ."

Nancy's eyes widened. Gold treasure hunter? Louis?

She shot a look at the handsome man, smiling as he drove the car. Suddenly, his words earlier played like a recording in her mind: "With sixty thousand dollars in 1878 gold coins at stake, who knows what could happen?"

She had never told Louis what she'd learned about how much the gold coins could be worth, she realized. He knew much more than he pretended to about Lizzie Applegate's treasure!

They had reached the pavilion. After parking the car, Louis asked the girls if they would carry in the last few curios from the trunk. They got out and went to the back of the car. Louis opened the trunk and lifted out two small cardboard boxes.

Nancy glanced inside the trunk. Her blood ran cold. Inside Louis's trunk was a red duffel bag.

"What is it, Nancy?" asked Louis suddenly. "You look like you've seen a ghost." His tone of voice was pleasant, but his eyes looked cold and hard. He laid his hand on the trunk lid and forcefully slammed it down.

Nancy faced Louis. Without more evidence, she knew she couldn't accuse him of causing the accidents. She just shook her head. "I'm fine," she said, and turned away.

Carrying boxes, the girls followed Abby and Hannah into the pavilion. Nancy could feel Louis's eyes boring into her back as he walked behind her.

The festivities had already begun inside. People strolled around the edges of the huge high-ceilinged room to visit the colorful booths and tables that lined its four sides. Holiday music filled the air, and many people wore costumes. As Nancy and the others made their way through the noisy crowd, Nancy saw an elf skip by followed by a fairy princess and then a vampire. On a small stage at one end of the square, children used long sticks to strike at a golden tasseled piñata overhead.

"Isn't this wonderful!" Bess cried.

Nancy nodded, but her mind was too full to enjoy the merriment. Louis had an old red duffel bag in his trunk. Tim had said "the old guy" left the mansion with a red duffel just before the fire. She'd assumed he meant Charlie. But what if it was Louis he saw?

Now that she thought about it, on the afternoon of the fire, Louis was already at the mansion when the others got there, but he hadn't called the fire department. Had he set Rose's letters on fire, then carried the old documents away? Were Lizzie's papers in that bag right now?

Rose was waiting for them at the Chandler Interiors booth. Out of the corner of her eye, Nancy saw Louis put his arm around Rose and kiss her under the mistletoe. His eyes gazed coolly at the crowd in the hall as he held Rose firmly.

Nancy shivered. She wondered why she hadn't suspected Louis before. Beneath the smooth, ever-ready smile was a man with tight control over Rose. A treasure hunter indeed, thought Nancy.

Louis leaned over to speak to Abby. Nancy quietly tilted her head, listening. "I made a phone call on my way in," she heard Louis tell Abby. "My mechanic looked at your car. The brakes are fine. He said they may have over-heated. Maybe Nancy was riding them too hard."

Nancy clenched her teeth. Louis was lying! Nancy had seen the severed brake lines herself.

With a nod, Nancy signaled to Bess and George to walk off with her. They walked past many booths, where artists and shop owners displayed quilts, ceramics, bead work, metal sculpture, and handmade ornaments. Once they were well away from Louis's booth, Nancy told the girls what she had just discovered.

"So Lizzie's treasure *is* at the heart of this case," Bess said. "Poor Rose. She really likes Louis."

Nancy nodded. "I know. But we have to prove Louis guilty before he hurts someone," she said.

"How?" asked George.

"We need to examine the red bag," Nancy said. "If Lizzie's papers are inside, we'll have good reason to believe Louis started the fire. We have to get into his car trunk."

The girls passed a booth with beautiful stained glass. Next to it was the Lees' booth, serving Chinese food. Mary waved at the girls. Wearing a red brocade robe and a matching headdress, she looked like a Chinese princess.

"What an amazing outfit, Mary," George said.

"Thanks," Mary said. "And look at the three of you. Those gowns look fabulous."

"I want a picture," Bess said. She posed Nancy, George, and Mary in front of the canvas backdrop of the Lees' booth, a painting of a Chinese pagoda. Then she asked Nancy to take a picture of her with Mary and George. George stepped away, and Nancy took another picture of Bess and Mary alone.

Nancy had just peeled back the paper from the third photograph when Hannah came up behind her. "Oh, let's see the picture," she said.

Nancy passed Hannah the snapshot of Mary and Bess in front of the pagoda.

Hannah scanned the photo. "Hunh!" Hannah said, nibbling at a fingernail. "There's something so familiar about this scene—Mary in her Chinese robe, Bess in her long gown and big hat, the pagoda behind them. . . . Oh, I know! It's that picture Bess showed me of Mary's great-grandfather and Lizzie in front of that Chinese mantel."

Nancy glanced at the photograph, then at Bess and Mary. Bess was tapping her toes and idly singing the song from *The Bandit's Treasure*, which she had been humming all day. " 'I'll wait for you by the Golden Gate and hold your treasure true,' " she sang. " 'Where the rainbow ends in Christmas gold and the phoenix rises, too.' "

Suddenly Nancy pictured the rainbow cast by the stained glass on the wall where the fireplace once was. Nancy imagined the Chinese mantel, with its rising phoenix, set in its original location over the fireplace. "Where the rainbow ends in Christmas gold and the phoenix rises, too."

Nancy quivered with excitement. "Hannah, you're a genius!" she shouted.

"I am?" Hannah looked perplexed.

"Yes," Nancy said. "Tell me: What do you find at the end of the rainbow?"

"Why, a pot of gold," Hannah answered.

"Right," Nancy said. "You've solved the mystery, Hannah!"

16

Yerba Buena Gold

"Lizzie's gold is buried in the mansion," Nancy whispered to George. "Just like in the song, it's at the end of the rainbow—a rainbow cast by the stained glass where the phoenix on the Chinese mantel once rose."

George gasped. "Nan, that's brilliant! Let's go find it."

"Find what?" Bess demanded, as she strolled over.

Nancy glanced at her watch. It was one-thirty. "No time to explain," she said quickly. "Bess, you and Hannah go back to the antiques booth. Try to keep Louis from leaving. And if he does leave, call me at the mansion. Call me at once!"

Outside, Nancy and George flagged a taxi that was just letting someone out. As it pulled up to them, Nancy frowned. It was a green-and-white car—a Bay City Cab. But luckily, Charlie wasn't driving it.

Nancy gave the driver the address of the mansion, asking him to hurry. Before she could stop him, he picked up his radio transmitter and told his location and destination to his dispatcher. She winced. In his cab, Charlie would hear the radio message and know that a cab was heading from the Winter Festival to the mansion on California Street. He might figure out that someone was onto him!

When the cab pulled up in front of the mansion, Nancy quickly paid the driver, and she and George jumped out. Barging through the front door, Nancy saw the rainbow on the blank wall. She placed her hand on the wall at the end of the rainbow. "The phoenix in the Chinese mantel used to sit right here, over the fireplace," she explained.

"But where is the gold?" George asked.

"The phoenix is supposed to rise from its own ashes," Nancy said.

"In the old fireplace!" George said excitedly.

"We need a tool to pry up the boards." Nancy snapped her fingers. "Charlie's tool kit." Holding her full skirt before her, Nancy ran to the saloon and returned with the tool kit. Using a chisel, she began prying up the floorboards.

Suddenly Nancy heard footsteps on the outside steps. Her heart jumped into her throat, and she whirled around.

Tim stuck his head in the front door. "I saw you run into the house," he said. "What's up?"

"A treasure hunt," George replied.

In a far corner under the boards, Nancy's groping hands touched something soft. She gave a tug and out came a canvas bag tied with rope. Her hands trembled excitedly as she untied the cord and held the bag upside down. Gold coins poured out.

Nancy picked up a coin. "Eighteen seventy-eight."

"The loot from the Christmas Day robbery," George said, clearly awed. "Christmas gold!"

At that moment the telephone in the office rang. Nancy leapt up and ran over to answer it.

"Nancy, it's Hannah," she heard the house-keeper's familiar voice. "Louis left the festival in a taxi ten minutes ago. I had to wait for a phone to call you."

Nancy's heart began racing again. Louis would be there any minute! "Thank you, Hannah." Nancy hung up the receiver and hurried back to the entry hall. "Louis is coming! Pack up the gold," she said to George and Tim. "And fast— we don't have much time. I'll call Lieutenant Chin."

Just then Nancy saw a shadow sneaking past the glass door at the rear of the entry hall. The door burst open. Charlie loomed in the doorway. He must have come in through the kitchen, Nancy realized.

Then the front door burst open, too. Louis stood there, a small silver gun in his hand. He no longer looked charming and polite. His eyes had hardened into a cold stare, and the corners of his mouth were pulled down.

"Run, Tim!" Nancy yelled. Tim sprinted past Charlie, ducking under his arms.

"Go after him!" Louis shouted. Charlie spun around and ran limping out after Tim.

Louis stared at the gold, his eyes gleaming, but he kept his gun pointed toward the girls. Nancy backed against the wall.

Charlie returned. "The kid got away."

Nancy silently breathed a sigh of relief. If Tim remembered what she'd said a moment earlier about calling Lieutenant Chin, she felt sure he would call the police. If she could just keep Louis talking until the police arrived! But she also needed a weapon, just in case. She began to fidget with the tiny bonnet perched on her head. If she could find the hatpin . . .

George saw Nancy's movements and understood at once. Still kneeling, George reached slowly for her hat on the floor beside her. George's fingers searched among the plumes and then stopped. George had found her hatpin now.

"So you were the other bidder on the mansion," Nancy said calmly to Louis, hiding the hatpin in the palm of her hand.

He sniffed and shrugged. "I was out of the country purchasing antiques when the mansion came up for sale," he said. "I'd been waiting for it for a couple of years. When I returned, I made an offer much higher than the asking price. But then Rose and Abby matched it."

147

"How did you figure out about the gold?" Nancy asked, playing for time.

Louis let loose a short, barking laugh. "A woman came to my store to sell a brooch—the emerald brooch your friend Bess admired so much. When I inquired about the brooch's history, the woman said her grandmother, Nellie Beecham, had been willed the brooch by Lizzie Applegate. She said her grandmother had told her stories of Lizzie's hidden treasure. I was already familiar with Lizzie's history. I was sure the treasure was here."

"So after Rose and Abby bought the house, you started creating the accidents," Nancy said.

"Yes," he replied. "With Charlie's help. In fact, it was Charlie who let me know you were here just now. He heard your driver on the cab radio and swung by the pavilion to let me know."

Nancy turned to Charlie. "It was you who cut the cords on the window so it would crash. You left the tap running that caused the flood. And you filed down the chandelier chain."

"Yeah," Charlie said gruffly, his face reddening. Nancy thought he seemed embarrassed.

"But why did you leave the file on the refrigerator?" George asked Charlie.

Charlie shrugged. "I took the chandelier to the kitchen to clean it—to wash the globes and crystal pendants. That's where I filed the chain. I'd just finished when Abby barged in and wanted to help. Since my tool kit was out in the entry, I just put the file on the refrigerator real quick, so she wouldn't see it. When I came back to the refrigerator for it the next day, it was gone."

Nancy nodded. Tim had taken the file that night to cut the cake. "You almost ran us down in the Presidio," she said to Charlie. "Why?"

"I asked Charlie to," Louis answered for Charlie. "When I dropped off the roses, I saw you two jogging toward the Presidio. I figured you needed to be discouraged somehow from your little detective efforts."

"You left the threatening note on the pillow," Nancy said to Louis.

"Yes," Louis said with a chilling smile. "The gardenia fragrance was a nice touch, don't you think? I hoped you would suspect Abby, since she has some gardenia perfume. I gave it to her myself."

"You cut the brake lines?" Nancy asked Louis.

Louis shook his head. "I had Charlie do that. I told him where you'd be. I had Cassandra make the phony call about Hannah."

"Cassandra?" Nancy asked. Had she helped with the sabotage too? Was that why she was so upset earlier when Nancy stopped by Louis's store?

"The day of the fire," George put in, "how did you get into the mansion?"

"I used Charlie's keys," Louis said. "I wanted to look at the historical documents while everyone else was out. But then I saw the ashes in the fireplace, and I remembered Rose's letters. So I started the fire." Louis began to look around. Nancy knew he was getting restless. When would the police get here?

"The fire turned out to be unnecessary," Louis went on. "Lizzie's papers told me nothing. How did *you* find the gold?" he said with a sneer.

Nancy kept silent. She wouldn't give Louis the satisfaction of knowing that the clue was in the song.

Now Louis became angry. "Tie them up!" he ordered Charlie.

"I'll get some rope," Charlie said, going to the back hall.

Nancy watched Charlie leave. With one man gone, she knew this was their chance. She lunged at Louis, using her hatpin to strike at his gun hand. With a quick leap, George stabbed Louis in the cheek with her hatpin, drawing blood.

"Ahhhhhhh!" he screamed, dropping the gun.

The girls tore across the hall in a rush of silk and taffeta. Louis was blocking the front door, and Charlie was in the back hall. The only way to go was down the saloon stairs. As they ducked that way, Nancy paused just long enough to pull the latch on the inside of the glass door. Nancy and George raced down the stairs into the dark saloon.

"The trapdoor," Nancy told George. "Take off your petticoat. You won't make it through the tunnel with that on." She heard a crashing noise above as Louis and Charlie began to batter at the locked door to the stairs.

Having hurriedly shed their huge petticoats, the girls crawled through the narrow tunnel to Tim's secret room. Safe for the moment, they turned and looked through the two-way mirror. They saw Louis and Charlie frantically search the saloon. Louis picked up Nancy's empty petticoat and gestured angrily. Then the men returned upstairs.

"Go up the ladder into the pantry," Nancy whispered. "But be totally quiet, okay?"

Nancy and George climbed to the pantry. Nancy spotted a fire extinguisher on the pantry wall. She pulled its pin and gave it to George. Then they grabbed another fire extinguisher from the back hallway.

Sirens sounded in the distance. "Let's get out of here," the girls heard Charlie say in the entry hall. "That blond kid must've called the police!"

"Do you have all the gold?" Louis said.

Now! Charging into the entry hall, the girls swung the fire extinguishers before them, spraying the men. Just then Nancy saw the front door open.

"Police!"

"I'll wait in Yerba Buena town,
in a house high above the sea."

Nancy, Bess, George, Mary, Tim, Rose, Hannah, and Emily all gathered around the piano

151

down in the saloon, singing while Abby played. At the end of the song, they clapped and cheered.

"Thank you, girls, for everything," Rose said. "You saved the mansion. You saved my dream."

"Hannah provided the most important clue," Nancy said. Hannah beamed.

"Lizzie's papers were found in the red duffel bag," Nancy reported. "I'm sorry about your letters, Rose. I'm afraid they're lost forever."

Rose smiled sadly. "I've accepted that now. And Louis's betrayal." With a plucky spirit, she lifted her chin. "Abby, I'd like to donate Lizzie's papers to the public library."

"Of course, Rose," Abby said.

"What will happen to Louis and Charlie?" Bess asked.

"I just spoke to Lieutenant Chin," Nancy answered. "Both men are in custody. The police will go easy on Charlie. Apparently, Cassandra once stole a valuable silver pendant from Louis's shop, and Louis used that to blackmail her and Charlie into helping him."

"We thought you were behind the accidents, Abby," George confessed.

"You were so mysterious," Bess said.

"I'm sorry," Abby said. "I needed to keep my magic tricks a secret to see if they would really work on an audience."

"I believed Lizzie's ghost was here," Bess murmured. "We saw her so many times. The blur in the photograph. The spirit at the séance. The figure in the mirror—but that was really you, Tim."

Rose turned toward the boy, who stood with his dog cradled in his arms. "Tim, now that Charlie's gone, we could use some extra help," she said. "We can't pay much, but you could live here at the mansion. Will you stay?"

"Will I?" Tim's blue eyes opened wide. "That's great! Thank you!" Tim hugged his dog to his chest. "Can Tramp stay, too?"

"Tramp, too," Rose said.

"As long as he doesn't chase Alfreida," Abby added with a teasing voice.

"Who gets the gold now?" asked Bess.

"The courts will decide who the bandit's treasure belongs to," Rose answered. "But the California Express Company people told me they will honor their old reward for finding it—three thousand dollars. This whole story has been great publicity for them."

"We can use the reward money to help renovate the mansion," Abby declared. "The Golden Gardenia will bloom again!" She struck a chord on the piano.

"Let's take a photograph," Bess said. "Everybody stand in front of the bar." Bess bustled around, posing everybody. "Perfect. Smile!" Bess snapped the picture.

A minute later Bess pulled back the film. Once again they saw a ghostly apparition in the background. "Lizzie?" Bess wondered. "What do you think, Emily?" She showed her the photograph.

Emily shook her head. "I have no idea what caused this, Bess. It really doesn't look like a reflection of light, I must say."

Just then the saloon lights flickered and the scent of gardenia seemed to waft through the air. Nancy shivered in spite of herself. She glanced over at Abby.

"Don't look at me," Abby said. "No tricks tonight."

"I *told* you guys," Bess insisted. "Lizzie's ghost *is* here."

Nancy smiled and shrugged. "It is weird, Bess," she admitted. "But I guess some mysteries are better left unsolved."

"And if a brilliant detective like Nancy Drew says that"—Rose laughed—"you know that it's true!"